The Awakening

Somewhere in the Eternal Darkness a shadow stirred. Its awakening, more than welcome, sent hot shivers of anticipation ripple through its very existence. It sighed and stretched, as though reaching out in search of a more tangible piece of evidence of what it could feel coming. The first taste of satisfaction came only what seemed like moments later. It savored that first taste, absorbing it slowly, with great pleasure and patience. As its consciousness grew so did its need. To just taste wasn't enough; it needed more. It needed to consume more, and it needed to do it faster. The hunger was strong and finally, coming fully awake, it lost all patience and greedily pulled at the Energy dancing around it, like a hungry animal devours its first kill. The Energy resisted, while it shimmered and sparkled, like small light explosions, as if unsure it should allow the darkness to caress it. Like new lovers, they danced, coming close, then withdrawing, each time giving hope that they would ultimately be together as one.

Time was meaningless.

And then, it could sense the Energy was growing tired of the dance, and it knew that soon the dance would be over. And when the dance ended the Energy would be swallowed into the Eternal Darkness forever.

A whisper floated on the heavy air.

Yes, come to me. So long, it's been so long.

Its hunger for the light became unbearable. Waiting had been long and painful, so it slept, ignoring the agonizing thirst. But now awake, with the very thing it craved beyond all else, pulsing in the darkness, it let the need take over and fed, ravenously. It sensed the Energy's weakness and pulled it into the hollow void where it lived. Offering no resistance the light swirled toward the shadow within a shadow as if being gathered by an unseen force. The sparkles of light popped and sparked as they swirled into a column that swayed and danced, opening up like a funnel, spreading into the vast sea of black. It rose up to consume the Energy, spreading its shadow into the darkness, pulling insistently. Suddenly, as if all resistance had vanished, the point of the funnel moved across the darkness, much the way a tornado weaves a path through the countryside, dodging and weaving, touching down to destroy anything in its path. But where a tornado leaves destruction, the Energy spread light—sparkling, intense, bursts of light. Radiant, pin sized points of light floating as if on a breeze. The shadow reached out and sparks touched its form, and disappeared into blackness.

Yes! Yes! Come to me!

The tip of the funnel followed into the darkness, letting the shadow caress its sparkling tip.

With a roar of triumph, the shadow drew the column of radiant light into its darkness, and rejoiced.

Chapter 1

With the approaching dawn, amber fingers of sunlight slipped through the crack in the heavy curtains to gently caress Dean's sleeping face. But it wasn't the light that penetrated Dean's heavy slumber. It was the annoying sound of a bee. A buzzing bee. Right beside his ear. No, *in* his ear. He swatted blindly with his hand, hoping he would by some stroke of luck manage to connect, sending the irritating pollen gatherer to insect heaven. Served it right, he thought with vengeance, hanging around where it wasn't wanted. He attempted another swat. No luck, the buzzing was constant and extremely disturbing. He stirred, and rolled over in frustration, one eye squinting open to peek at the clock on his night table. It was then that he realized that the bee had arms and they said it was six–thirty. He groaned, slapped the SNOOZE button, rolled onto his back and closed his eyes. *Just five more minutes*, his sleepy mind begged.

One hour later Dean woke up.

He scrambled out of bed and stumbled down the hall and into the black and white tiled bathroom. It reminded him of the checkered flag at the race track. He guessed that was the point, given that John, his foster dad, was a racing fan. It might not have been so bad, but the orange stripe, orange bath mat, orange shower curtain and orange GAS STOP sign was over the top. Actually it was downright nauseating first thing in the morning. Running cold water into the sink, he cupped his hands to catch some and splashed his face. Somewhat refreshed, he raised his face to look into the mirror. A jolt of surprise coursed through him and he instinctively jumped back, knocked into the wall behind him, and reached out at the same time. He stepped forward to touch the mirror. Rivulets of water traced their way to the edge of the mirror and dropped into the sink. His other hand grabbed the edge and popped open the door. Dean leaned his head out, looking quizzically at the numerously sized and shaped bottles lining the shelves, then with the same puzzled expression turned to check the back of the mirror to see what was wrong with it.

What the…..?

"Dean!! Are you up?" a voice from below yelled in tones high enough to shatter glass. "Dean!!" the voice screeched again. "Get yer butt outta bed and get down here. Now!"

Dean grimaced. "Coming." He hollered, more at the mirror than at the voice downstairs. No time to figure it out now. The voice would only get louder and higher pitched if he didn't get moving.

The voice was Dean's foster mom, a short, bony woman with exaggerated troll-like features. All she needed to finish off the look were two pointed ears. Dean sometimes wondered if she really did have them but kept them somehow hidden. Her skin always had this sickly tint of green, probably from the three-pack a day habit she had. Short tufts of flat brown hair rudely stood up all over her head. She stood in the kitchen in her too-pink terry towel housecoat boasting blue trim, with a cigarette hanging out of her pinched, wrinkled mouth. "Bout time you hauled yer butt down here. Whadda ya think, yer on holidays or somethin'?"she sneered. She turned and butted her cigarette into a large, black, glass ashtray already holding the three cigarette butts from earlier in the morning.

Dean wordlessly moved to the cupboard.

"Not likely Deanny boy. You ain't got time for breakfast. Next time git up on time! I don't know how many times I told you not to stay up late readin' them stupid books of yours. No wonder ya can't get up in the mornin'. Now git going!" She threw his backpack at him, another sneer deforming her hollow boned cheeks and her sharp, sunken eyes daring him to challenge her, and motioned him out the door impatiently with one bony hand while the other lit up another cancer stick.

Dean banged out the door, letting the screen door rebound off the jam, and feeling a sense of pleasure as the troll inside the house hollered, "And quit lettin' that door slam like that!" He bounced down the stairs and along the sidewalk toward the gate. Reading was one thing Dean wasn't going to give up, especially for that, that .... poor excuse for a person. A memory tried to surface and Dean successfully pushed it back. It was much safer to keep them there. Much safer.

The usual golden marigolds and purple lobelia should have lined the sidewalk, the lawn should be neatly trimmed, the rose should be climbing the trellis over the gate and the fence should be freshly painted. Instead, various weeds grew in a tangled mass along the sidewalk, the lawn was dotted with dandelions and although the rose was climbing over the trellis, it just didn't look as good. But then, John was the gardener, the repairman and the renovator and.....gone.

As Dean slammed through the gate he glanced back at the place he now called home. The white duplex was definitely showing the signs of John's absence. John was the troll's husband, up until six months ago, when he walked out the front door and never returned. He never even bothered to say goodbye to Dean or come back for his stuff. Just walked out and never looked back. Dean wished he could do that. Walk out and never come back. Dean was never sure about what John had seen in his trollish wife. They were so different.

John was a gentle giant, standing about six foot four and weighing in at about two hundred and fifty pounds. His just-past-the-shoulder length hair was always pulled back in a ponytail and his thick arms sported several detailed tattoos, enhancing his I-could-be-a-biker image.

Two snakes wound their way from wrist to bicep, almost appearing to move when John flexed the massive bulk of his right arm. It was a trick that usually sent little girls screaming to their mothers and put wide grins on the faces of little boys. But the snakes weren't Dean's favorite tattoo. No, the tattoo that captured Dean's interest was the intricate dragon engulfed in flames. It started about his mid back and reached to the top of his left shoulder blade. The flames encased the dragon and licked their way over John's shoulder. He was usually a bit mysterious about why he picked that particular tattoo. But one day when Dean and John were out working in the yard together Dean asked the question once again. "John, what made you get a tattoo of a dragon?"

Surprisingly, John leaned in close and whispered cryptically, "One day Dean you will know the answer to that question but I won't be the one to give it to you." John then continued to trim the edges of the grass with his nifty new Black and Decker trimmer.

From the outside John looked like someone who could snap you in half with two fingers and not even break a sweat. But Dean knew different. Dean knew John from the inside. And on the inside John was kind and patient and always there to help you and listen if you had a problem. When Dean did something stupid, and Dean did plenty of those lately, John didn't yell and hit or make Dean feel stupid. John was always good about talking to him and helping him work things out. It was Janet, the troll, who was always screaming in the background, threatening to get rid of him, threatening to beat him or threatening to lock him in his room.

And now here he was. John was gone and he was still here. Again Dean wished he could do what John had done.

But of course he couldn't. Where would he go? If only....if only what? Dean said to himself. What? If only things were the way they used to be? Used to be long ago? Or used to be six months ago? Either way it's done, it's over and you have to move on and just make the best of it. So quit feeling sorry for yourself and get to school or you'll have something else to deal with that you don't need. It's only one week until school's out and then freedom! Summer holidays. Long days and even longer nights to do nothing, absolutely nothing. Unless Janet, the troll, manages to come up with a ton of chores, which of course she will, Dean reminded himself. And there's that little problem of the mirror, what could.......?

"Dean! Hurry up, man. We're gonna be late!" Tom, Dean's best friend, yelled from the top of the school steps. Dean took the steps two at a time. This morning would have to wait. No time for crazy stuff now.

The bell went seconds before Tom and Dean came to a skittering slide around the corner right into Mr. Desdale, the vice principal. He stepped back to avoid the collision. "Well, well, late again, Mr. Albany? I'm not surprised. It would have been a record if you had managed to go through the week without a tardy on your attendance record." Mr. Desdale stated with more than a little disdain. The effort wrinkled the brow on his hawkish face. "But I am surprised at the company you manage to keep." He continued, his dark, beady eyes moving to rest pointedly on Tom. "Someday, young Tom, this boy," he gestured to Dean, "is going to get you into trouble. You should be more careful who you make friends with."

Mr. Desdale seemed to be making it his personal life mission to catch Dean doing something wrong. His tall, angular figure patrolled the halls dressed in the only clothes Dean had ever seen him wear. Dean wondered if he had multiple black suits, white crisp shirts and shiny black shoes or if Desdale did his laundry every night, meticulously cleaning his dark suit, pressing those sharp creases into the legs, making sure all the buttons were secure on his always-buttoned jacket and applied starch to his crisp, white shirt. Or did his wife do it for him? Would a guy like Desdale have a wife? A memory, like a pinpoint of light, flashed in the back of Dean's mind. He snuffed it out without mercy.

Tom opened his mouth to tell Mr. Desdale that he knew very well how to pick his friends and that Dean was a good friend, better than most, thank you very much. But Dean read his friend's cold brown eyes and cut him off. "Sorry Mr. Desdale, real sorry. It was my fault. I slept in. I promise it won't happen again. Can we go to class now?" The question was asked with just enough innocence that Mr. Desdale had to look twice to make sure Dean was being sincere. The kid was nothing but trouble. "Well, you better get off before you miss half your English class," he growled. Then he swept past them as if they didn't exist. Off to patrol more near empty hallways.

"You didn't have to take the rap for me," Tom scolded his buddy. "I have a mind of my own. I could have gone on to class without you. Besides, Mr. Desdale has no right to talk to you like that. Why don't you tell him off? Or tell someone? It makes me want to take that pointed nose of his and smash it flat."

The thought of Mr. Desdale with a flat nose made Dean smile. "Geez Tom. Venting some of your pent up hostilities? Not that the idea doesn't have appeal." They stopped at the door of English class, looked knowingly at each other, and stepped inside.

They both received break detentions. Mrs. Temple gave them her *when you're late you miss the most important part of class* speech and then told them to stay put for break and get caught up. Even at her sternest ,Mrs. Temple was a joy for the eyes.

Dean figured that most of the grade nine boys had a crush on her. She was soft voiced and a real looker. But it wasn't what she looked like that made Dean appreciate his English teacher. It was her sense of fairness. She always dealt with the students fairly. No matter who they were they were dealt with in the same way. Mrs. Temple always treated Dean respectfully, even when he was in trouble. That was what made her different. Dean just plain liked her.

Bzzzzzzzz! The lunch bell sounded. Good, Dean though. I gotta go so bad!

The students spilled out into the hallways. On his trip to the washroom Dean spotted Tom. "Yo,hey, Tom! Yo!"

Tom jostled through the sea of bodies. "What's your hurry?" he said as he quickened his pace to keep up.

"Gotta go. Didn't want to leave class, but now I gotta go!"

"Ohhh, your back teeth are floating hey?" Tom joked.

Dean pushed through the door into the bathroom and ran into the last guy in line. "Ah darn, there's a line. Wouldn't you know it? There's never a lineup in the guys' washroom. It's always the girls' washroom that has a line up down the hall."

The boy in front moved ahead. Dean tried to concentrate on something other than his full bladder. He looked to his left and almost jumped back into Tom. The mirrors over the sinks were directly in line with him. For one second Dean scrutinized the faulty mirror, then, his gaze shifted to quickly check the other mirrors in the room. Nope, just his. Fear spiked its way up his spine making him jerk back and into Tom.

"Hey! What are you doing man? Hey, where are you going?" Tom called out as he left the line to follow his buddy. "Dean! Hey! What the.... Dean!"

Dean hurried down the hall towards the front doors of Central High. A sense of panic was growing at a rate that had Dean needing fresh air and completely forgetting his full bladder. He pushed past someone, not noticing anything around him, just intent on getting outside where he could breathe.

"Hey! Butt crack!! Watch where you're going!" the guy yelled.

Dean didn't even hear him. He was moving through the crowd of people as fast as he could with little to no regard for manners. His shoulder rammed another person hard enough to knock them back a step. This time it was the wrong person. Denis Levine, or Denis the Menace, the biggest bully in the school. A large, fat hand grabbed Dean by the scruff of his shirt and hauled him back a step or two. Dean suddenly realized that not only was he not moving forward anymore but his feet were not on the floor. He dangled like a rag doll by his armpits. A monster with a round, fat face, two beady eyes, and large lips that spit when they spoke, stared at him as if it expected something.

"I said... don't you watch where you're goin? I think you need to learn some manners... *geek*." The last word was said with emphasis and the rounding of beady eyes.

Dean finally realized he was in trouble. Of course, at a time like this, Desdale was nowhere to be found.

"Maybe a trip to the bathroom and a head dunkin'" would wake you up? Hey, geek? Hey?" Denis sneered then laughed. Everyone went quiet and stepped back. No one would challenge Denis the Menace. Besides, the kid did bump into him and almost knock him down. He should watch where he was going. Right? Denis started towards the washrooms dragging Dean along with him. Dean struggled against the iron grip holding onto his shirt collar but the fat hand only squeezed tighter. The sea of bodies parted as they made their way down the hall towards the boys' bathroom door. The kids started to laugh and point. Denis swept past Tom, who did a double take as Dean also swept past him with a look of terror on his face as he stumbled along in his attempt to keep up with his captor. Denis banged through the bathroom door and yelled, "Everybody out! I got business in here! This dolt needs a dunkin'….a serious dunkin! EVERYBODY OUT!!"

The bathroom emptied in seconds. Denis hauled Dean up in front of him by the scruff of his neck. His red, puffy face, too close, he sneered, "Well, well, well, look at that, no one's around. You pathetic, scrawny weakling, you need a lesson in manners don't you? Nobody knocks into me and gets away with it. Not some bony geek like you! Look at you, you're just a pencil, man! Don't you eat?" Denis shook Dean like a rag doll and turned him to face the mirrors. "Look at yourself! Loo….!"

Dean's head snapped up. In the mirror he could see the puzzlement in Denis' face turn to horror and then to fear. The fat hand lost its grip on Dean's shirt leaving Dean standing before the mirror with a million thoughts running through his mind. The Menace had turned pale and was backing out the door when Tom came bursting in.

"Your friend's a freak man. Just keep him away from me, or I'll toss both of you in a garbage dumpster," he threatened as he backed out of the bathroom, his eyes still riveted to the opposite wall. "I mean it."

The threat lost power when the Menace's voice cracked and he wiped a bead of sweat from his now ashen white forehead.

Tom was totally not getting it. Dean should be head first in a grungy toilet by now, screaming for help. Instead, he was standing alone before the row of mirrors with a somewhat perplexed look on his face.

"Hey man, how'd you do that? And how come Denis thinks you're a freak?" Tom questioned.

Dean remained silent, just staring ahead at the mirror. Then suddenly he yelled, "BECAUSE I AM!" and bolted past Tom, out the door, through the crowd and ran towards the woods, his mind racing with possibilities. *It's not possible, it's not possible.* He kept repeating the phrase as if by doing so it would make it the truth. *I can't be, but what else makes any sense? It's just not possible.* Dean slowed his pace as he reached the edge of the woods by the river. His fingers ran over his neck, searching, probing, and found nothing. He looked up toward the sun and squinted. No, no sensitivity there. *Then what? What the hell was going on?!*

Tom arrived breathless. "What the hell is wrong with you man?!" Tom's words mirrored Dean's thoughts. "Dean!! Answer me!"

Dean turned to face his friend, a sick look in his blue eyes. There was no other explanation. "I'm a vampire."

Chapter 2

Tom looked at his friend as if he had suddenly grown two heads. His serious, ebony eyes narrowed slightly and his head tilted to one side as Tom continued to assess Dean's face, as if looking for some hidden clue.

"I wonder if a vampire bat bit me during the night or something?" Dean worried aloud, still tossing ideas around in his head in a desperate attempt to rationalize what was happening.

Tom's eyebrows rose and he finally said, "You're kidding, right? This is a joke." Then added, "Jeez, Dean, you're gonna get us in big trouble on the last week of school. This is not a very funny joke. Man, I'm gonna miss class!" Tom shook his head as he turned to start back to the school.

Tom had been Dean's best friend from the moment the two met, over two years ago. Dean moved into the foster home in mid August. It was hot and sultry, the air heavy with the scent of the herbs the lady next to the basketball court grew in her little garden patch just off the back kitchen door. Tom was shooting hoops, his back drenched in sweat, when the blue sedan drove up and the woman in the gray suit got out. Tom remembered wondering how that lady could wear so many clothes on a day when the air seemed to just hang, without so much as a whiff of movement. Her outfit was crisp and tailored to her shape. Blond hair, dark at the roots, was pulled back in a swirl and held in place with a black clip that looked somewhat like a butterfly. Her expression was sober and as she clipped along the sidewalk in her sturdy high heels she tried to smile at Dean, but the tight smile didn't quite reach her eyes. Tom was curious about the new boy arriving at the Harpers, the fourth kid in two years. No one ever seemed to stay in that house very long. When Dean got out of the car he looked up and saw Tom. His sad eyes locked on Tom's face. Tom smiled.

Dean's mouth smiled back but his eyes remained sad, haunted. Tom held up the basketball in invitation and mouthed *later*. Dean nodded and followed the lady in the gray suit into the white duplex. A couple of hours later the blue car drove away and Tom knocked on the door. The heat of the day was subsiding so the two boys played one on one for a couple of hours. The rest of that hot, humid summer the two boys were inseparable and spent the remaining days of the summer hanging out together. Since that day Dean had shared some of his life but not much. And Tom discovered that Dean could be difficult to understand sometimes. He often did things that Tom just couldn't go along with. Like last weekend. He was really going to walk the rail on the bridge. Just so he could impress some jerks who dared him. Dean was spitting mad when Tom pulled him down and hauled him off.

As Tom dragged him away Dean struggled and shouted, "An idiot could walk that rail! Let me go, Tom! Let me go!"

But Tom held fast to his buddy's shirt and continued away from the scene. "You got no right interfering! Mind your own business!!"

Tom returned with, "Only an idiot would *try* to walk the rail!" and kept dragging his buddy away, all the while a vision of Dean, broken and bloody on the rocks below, playing itself in his frustrated mind. The river was low this time of year, revealing the treacherously sharp and deadly boulders that lined the riverbed. Plenty of people had fallen to their death off this bridge. When the water was high early in the spring or summer season it looked innocent enough, but those who lived in the area knew the dangers hidden beneath the inviting swirling liquid. No, it wasn't the drop from the bridge to the water that was the issue, it was the unseen peril hidden by cool waters. That's why Tom was so mad. Dean could plainly see where he would land if he fell. And still he chose to take the dare. It was as if he had a death wish!

"You're making me look like a fool! Let me go! They'll think I was chicken!" Dean hollered. "They're friends of mine. It's just for fun."

"Friends don't get friends to do something that could kill them! They're not your friends! All they care about is getting a good laugh at your expense! What's up with you? Have you lost your mind?" Tom yelled back as he shook his friend loose and let him fall onto his butt in front of him.

Rage turned Dean's blue eyes to ice and he slowly got to his feet. Through clenched teeth he ground out, "You had no right. It was my choice." His body shook with barely contained rage but he turned and walked away.

"Your choice to die? I don't think so my friend," Tom muttered under his breath. He had seen that fury before and knew just how long it would take Dean to cool off and call him. But he would call. Tom could count on it.

And now this?

"Come on, the bell is gonna go any minute."

Dean stood rooted to the ground, his hands clenched in knuckle-white fists that came up to either side of his face. Fear and frustration exploded. "I'm not kidding!!" he screamed. "I'm serious!! Do I look like I'm playing a joke on you?!" he screamed. "I'm telling you I think I'm a vampire.

Tom froze. He had never seen Dean like this, this hysterical, angry yes, but not like this. A small spike of alarm found its way up Tom's spine. Okay, so ask the burning question. "Why do you think you're a vampire?"

Relief flooded Dean's mind. He desperately needed Tom to believe his story. Tom was a slightly built Chinese boy with straight black hair and serious eyes of ebony. That's how he dealt with life....seriously, and his oriental heritage lent him an air of tradition and wisdom. Tom was always spouting tidbits of insight he learned from his grandfather. In Dean's world of uncertainty Tom's beliefs gave him a sense of stability Dean desperately needed. What could Tom know about fear, or acceptance? His family had roots in the water front city of Trinity that went clear back to his great grandfather. And he was Dean's best and only friend. Yeah, Dean needed Tom, needed him to believe what he was about to see.

"Come on and I'll show you."

The two silently made their way through the empty halls glancing over their shoulders repeatedly and checking corners and extending hallways with the caution of two spies on a secret mission. They didn't want to run into Mr. Desdale again, or anyone else for that matter. Finally they pushed the door to the boys' washroom open. Dean came to an abrupt halt directly in front of one of the many mirrors lining the wall. He motioned with this hand for Tom to come closer. "Well? What do you see?"

Tom looked into the mirror. "Nothing," he said frankly. "Absolutely nothing."

His hand reached out to touch the mirror.

"Don't bother. Believe me I've tried that. Well, what do you think? Could I be a vampire?" Dean said, tipping his head back and baring his teeth for inspection.

Tom was still inspecting the mirror. He looked again but all he could see reflected in the mirror was the tiled wall and shiny white urinals that lined the other side of the bathroom.

No Dean. But he was standing right there! He reached out and touched the blond curls he had teased Dean about so many times, as if touching them might somehow reinstate their reflection. His hand appeared alone, suspended in mid air. He looked back at his friend with his head back and his mouth wide open. "Don't be crazy. There is no such thing as vampires," Tom reasoned with great certainty.

Dean dropped his head.

"Then what?"

Tom looked thoughtful and then said, "I don't know what's wrong, but I know someone who will."

Chapter 3

A small, tarnished brass bell tinkled as Tom opened the ancient, carved door and stepped inside the shop.

So this was Tom's great-grandfather's emporium. Dean had always wondered what it looked like. He glanced around the dark room, noting the shelf-lined walls cluttered with various jars and boxes and large glass top counters filled with things Dean could only image the names of. The air had an unfamiliar sweet scent that Dean found pleasant. Tom didn't talk about his great-grandfather very much but when he did his tone usually became hushed and mysteriously reverent. Tom believed his great-grandfather to be an ancient wizard with the special powers of nature. Dean never put much store in the stories but never discouraged his buddy from telling them. Tales of magic and promise were something Dean gave up believing some time ago.

An incredibly old, oriental man, small in stature and somewhat bent in posture, raised his head to peer towards the sound of the brass bell as the two boys entered. He'd been waiting for them to arrive, wondering if his great-grandson's friend would finally find his way to his destiny. His dream last night was vivid, but not all Mao's dreams came true, vivid or not. Life can be so unpredictable, and this youngster had experienced more than his share of the uncertainties life can deliver.

Tom's image had appeared first, his serious brown eyes especially serious and full of frustration. He was arguing with someone. A blond boy, a friend, someone he cared about. Tom was pulling this friend along by his shirt and muttering under his breath. The two boys were on the Port Mann Bridge, at the top of the span, with a group of kids just a short distance away. The kids were laughing and pointing. Tom seemed oblivious to them and to their comments and was focused on the boy he had in tow. The kid's energy aura sparkled and shimmered around them, bright with life, as only the young can. When the blond boy's energy aura suddenly disappeared, and the space around him turned dull and empty, Mao bolted upright on his simple, single-mattress bed. A familiar ripple shivered its way through the air, disturbing Mao enough that he got up, made tea, and planned what he would do when his grandson brought his blond-haired friend to him.

~~~~~~

Dean was facing a short old man with long, wispy white hair that hung to the same length as his white beard and mustache, which was just a ruler's length away from brushing the floor. He parted a curtain of wooden beads hanging in the doorway and stepped into the room. His slight frame suggested fragility until one looked into his coal black eyes. Spirit and strength sharpened his glance, a strength born only to the soul. Wrinkles wove a map of years upon his kind face. He wore traditional black mandarin garb, the only thing unusual being the intricately embroidered design along the lapels. Peacock blue dragons rode shockingly white lightning bolts. The dragons were laughing and playing, as if one with the electrical rod they rode. Gold smoke swirled from their nostrils and silver flames spewed from their mouths and licked the edges of the lapels.

Dean wondered what it meant.

Tom knew. He bowed briefly, almost imperceptibly. "Great-grandfather."

Mao looked directly at Dean, his black eyes bottomless pits filled with wisdom. Dean shivered and instantly understood the awe Tom felt for this dynamic old man. His eyes burned to Dean's very soul. Dean could feel the searing heat and felt a sharp need to withdraw.

"You are very unfortunate boy," he stated in English laced heavily with an oriental accent. "You have no soul."

"I have no reflection," Dean corrected him.

"Same thing," The old man returned matter-of-factly. "You have big problem."

Dean took that step back. "What do you mean? Of course I have a soul. That's a terrible thing to say!"

"No reflection, no soul," Mao repeated. There was no room to argue with his tone.

Dean turned to Tom, his eyes wide with a mixture of fear and disbelief. Fear put one step toward the door. Disbelief another. Tom reached out to touch Dean's shoulder, to support, but also to stay his retreat.

"Great-grandfather," Tom applied pressure to the suddenly shaking shoulder under his grasp. "Could you please explain what you mean? We do not understand. How could Dean lose his soul?"

The old man slowly moved to a shelf and removed a jar. The aroma of something familiar and yet, not, assaulted Dean's nostrils. He dipped his hand into the jar and said, "Your friend not own his mind. Everybody own his mind but him."

What? Own my mind? Of course I own my mind, it's mine isn't it? What a ridiculous thing to say. Dean ignored that familiar tug at the back of his mind.

"Lose my soul, don't own my mind, none of this makes sense." Dean scoffed, then, turned towards the door. "I'm outta here."

Mao continued to remove handfuls of the substance in the jar and place it in a paper bag. Not a word was spoken but Dean sensed himself being pulled toward the old man. He spun around as if some unknown force had taken him by the shoulders and physically turned him. Fear widened his clear blue eyes, but he continued to move toward the old man against his will. Finally, he was standing directly in front of the old wizard, his blue eyes as round as saucers.

"You see, very easy to make you do something you don't want to."

Dean couldn't believe what he was hearing. The old wizard actually expected him to believe that he made Dean move! A strong aroma washed over Dean again. Curiosity had him asking, "What is that?" Probably magic herbs or incense or something equally weird Dean expected.

"Tea," Mao answered, folding the top of the bag over.

Dean felt dumb, not to mention insulted by Mao Tsu's description of his character. But if Dean was really honest with himself he would have to admit the old man hit the nail on the head. That's what made this whole experience even scarier. Dean never could resist trying to impress or fit in with the "IN" crowd. He always did what everyone else wanted, at least it seemed that way. And every time he did he would get that tug, that familiar tug in the back of his mind that would make him believe, if only for a moment, that he didn't have to do what they wanted, that he was good enough. And Dean would push it away, not able to believe it. So this is where it got him. Great, now what?

"Is there any way I can get it back?"

"Or ....is it too late?" Tom joined in, voicing his fear for his best friend. Tom had never seen Dean stand up to pressure from others and he had this wild sense that it was too late, way too late.

Too late? A shot of apprehension had Dean jerking back and he closed his eyes, fearful of the answer.

"Too late?" Mao repeated.

Dean's heart dropped to his feet along with his chin.

"It's never too late," the ancient wizard finished.

Dean's eyes popped open with surprise and his head snapped up, causing one stray lock of curly, blond hair to fall across his tanned forehead.

"But," Mao cautioned, "The path is long and filled with risk and danger. One must be very determined and brave. The faint of heart will fail at the tasks required."

Dean's heart sank again.

"I will help him great-grandfather. He can do it. I know he can." Tom turned to Dean. "You've got to try! What have you got to lose?"

Dean struggled with his fear and doubts. It was like there was a war going on inside him. Easy for Tom to say. What would he know about fear? An image of the past reared its head to mock Dean's attempt at courage. Its hideous, cruel laughter taunted him. Teasing him to try... and fail. Usually Dean listened to its taunts and believed them, then would shove it back into the box he had so carefully placed it in so many years ago... and wait for the next time.

"He does not have the strength," Mao bated, sensing the struggle Dean was attempting to win. "He cannot reach deep enough to even start the journey. He must be able to step into the Darkness to find the Light."

Dean's fear turned into anger, anger and resentment for all the pain he had lived with for the last two years. Anger because this wise man saw his fear, recognized it, expected Dean to cave to it, and wasn't even disappointed. As if it were destiny for Dean to live the rest of his life like this.... afraid. Well, not this time. Not this time! Dean's blue eyes had turned the shade of glacier ice and were just as cold. He looked Mao straight in the eye and said, "What do I have to do?"

Mao stroked the length of his beard while he assessed the boy before him. A spark twinkled back at him from those frosty blue eyes, a spark that hadn't been there when the young man had entered his shop. He would need it. He would need all the strength he possessed to complete the journey he was about to embark on. Mao had his doubts whether the boy could do it but he had to let him try.

"Follow me."

Mao passed through another curtain of wooden beads, into the small room at the back of the shop. With his bony hands clasped together, he bowed his head. Then, he raised his hands, as if in worship of some unknown force. Suddenly he stood before a beautiful mural of an ancient door. The patterns in the painting were the same as the dragons embroidered on Mao's black lapels. The room became thick with static, small shards of blue light shot from Mao's fingertips. The mural slowly transformed from a one dimensional painting to a rich, thickly carved door that smelled of the exotic wood of which it had been crafted.

Dean was dumbfounded.

Tom looked as if some wonderful secret had been revealed.

"Come, come," Mao waved. The door, perhaps a foot thick, slowly opened to reveal darkness.

Dean hesitated briefly but lost the choice when Tom shoved him from behind into the darkened room. As Mao stepped into the small chamber the ancient door closed with a solid thud, encasing them in total darkness. Before the boys could react Mao lit a wall candle, then another and another and when he was done the room was bathed in soft, flickering light.

Beautifully woven tapestries, rich with ancient tales, draped the walls; the short spaces of brick between bore the candle holders. In the center of the room was a small table. Several strange things were scattered across its slab. Things Dean had no idea about.

Shelves, filled with jars of varying shapes and sizes, lined one wall. These jars were nothing like the jars in the outside shop. These were ancient, inscribed jars. Their contents could make a less squeamish person tremble. Live, squirming, slender snakes slipped and slithered their paths through the water in one jar. Large bodied spiders with long, hairy, black legs skittered around another. Lizard Tongue, Wart Toad Intestines, the jars went on and on, the next one equally or more disturbing than the one before it.

The old man bent over and took hold of a latch that hadn't been there seconds before. It was as though the suggestion of touching it created its presence. The hinges of the ancient trap door screeched in protest as Mao opened it fully. He turned to the boys.

"This," the old man pointed to the hole in the floor, "is the UnderWorld of Darkness."

Tom's eyes rounded to wide pools of ebony. He remained silent but his mind was flying through all the tales and legends he'd heard as a child about the UnderWorld of Darkness. It was a world filled with danger and strange creatures, but the legend states that if you successfully navigate its perils you will reach the InnerWorld of Light. The most prized possession anyone could ever have. Tom never did know what exactly the InnerWorld of Light was, but seeing as everyone wanted it he figured it had to be worthwhile. The legends told of lost souls entering the UnderWorld of Darkness never to return. The legends also told of lost souls returning with the InnerWorld of Light and their lives changing forever.

Mao continued," Are you sure you can do what is needed?"

"What.....what is needed?" Dean hesitantly questioned, his eyes locked on the dark opening. A thin sliver of fear caused his voice to crack.

"During your journey through the Darkness you must retrieve three important articles. The Longgu Oracle, a spiritual script carved by the ancients on the shell of a tortoise and laid in fire to reveal its truth. Heed the ancient language, it foresees your path and warns of the perils of darkness. The Flaming Pearl, an amulet of luck that symbolizes wisdom. Most importantly, the Liquid Mirror of Mie-Self. It will be the most difficult to retrieve, and the most important. Its power is nothing I can speak of or describe, but for you to discover on your own," Mao stated mysteriously. "You will need to trust your instincts and follow your heart. And you will need help, for each of them is guarded by The Spirit of the Way, which creates eternal change."

Tom's eyes rounded and he opened his mouth to speak. No sound was possible. He tried once again. Panic spiked its way into his heart, stopping it. His eyes darted toward Mao. The wizard's ebony eyes pinned him and silently warned him to stay his course. Tom clamped his mouth shut. Then, he tentatively cleared his throat. Pointedly, his great-grandfather raised his right brow, and turned away. Mao moved to the shelf that contained jars labeled Unicorn Horn, Faery Wing, and Pixie Dandruff. He reached for a shiny silver box, opened it to reveal a small shiny orb, about the size of the palm of your hand, and placed it on the square table in the center of the room. Carefully he stepped around the darkness on the floor and moved toward another shelf with jars labeled Feverfew, Devil's Claw, and Angelica. He stretched up to the top shelf and removed an ancient wooden carved box, flipped it open, to reveal what appeared to be a bean. The kind of bean he'd helped John plant in the garden last summer. What magical property could a bean have? Mao laid it next to the opened silver box and turned. The old man's eyes were black with intensity as they looked pointedly at Dean. "You must find your way to the Chamber of Souls. You will need strength and courage to confront your demons at the gate, but if you succeed you will retrieve your soul."

Dean cringed inwardly, secretly wishing he could return the old man's stare with equal intensity. But of course he couldn't. His eyes dropped to the floor.

"He cannot follow the path. He is too weak," Mao said bluntly.

Dean's head popped up and he looked fearfully at Tom. Tom smiled reassuringly. "Yes, he can great-grandfather. I know he can."

Dean's grateful gaze met Tom's.

Tom's right. Dean thought. *I can do it. Tom's always right. Why would it be any different now?*

The old man viewed the exchange. He shrugged. He opened the long, slender box that suddenly lay across the palms of his hands. Cradled in white velvet, a long, slender crystal sparkled. A kaleidoscope of iridescent colors danced within its beauty. In that moment, Dean believed the world's secrets were held captive within the crystal's essence and he wanted to learn some of those secrets.

"Listen carefully. These," Mao gestured to the objects now also suddenly together on the table next to their containers, "are your three charms. The Silver Orb, the Living Bean and the Iyc Crystal. They will help you complete your tasks if used wisely. I cannot tell you how to use them, that is up to you. Be careful of where you plant the Living Bean, as your thoughts are reflected in its growth. Thoughts can be treacherous." Mao's eyes narrowed as he leaned into Dean's face. "Beware.......your path may not always be obvious but it is always before you. Your task is one of great risk and you must always remember, the fire of the soul turns to ice when unused," Mao warned mysteriously. He leaned closer still and continued, "To find true self one must sometimes sacrifice that which keeps them safe."

He placed the three objects into an electric blue velvet pouch with a silver strap and held it out to Dean. Dean put the strap over his shoulder Robin Hood style and took a deep breath.

"The UnderWorld of Darkness calls your name." Mao gestured to the darkness below and stepped aside.

Chapter 4

The ancient trap door closed with a heavy, ominous thud, leaving the two boys encased in total darkness. A darkness known only to someone who has been in the wilderness on a overcast night, with no cast of the moon to lend light, no stars, nothing but an inky black void. Darkness so intense a person wouldn't see their hand in front of their face. City or town dwellers would never know such darkness. Streetlights chase away the shadows and houses glow with the light of life.

In the blackness, the outside world ceased to exist. The only sound was the music of water rivulets trickling their way down the walls of the tunnel with perfectly timed droplets falling from the roof to plunk in unseen puddles below. It was a moment frozen in time for both boys. Dean pulled in a deep breath of heavy, dank air laced with an odor that jabbed at his memory.

"Dad, it smells in here," eight year old Dean complained, as he wrinkled his nose in distaste. "Why does it smell so wet?"

"Because the ground is sort of leaking water all the time so everything stays wet. The rock is limestone and has been here millions of years. The water has added mineral deposits as it runs over the rock leaving these very cool shapes." Dean's father explained, with a smile on his face and encouragement in his voice.

"Dean?" Tom whispered, the hushed expression echoing slightly. "Can you see anything?"

Dean shook the memory away. "Can you?" he answered in a tone that implied how ridiculous the question was.

This is it. No turning back now.

You'll never do this. You don't have what it takes. Turn back, before it's too late. Don't worry, Tom will understand. Dean pushed the familiar voice into an imaginary wall. Slamming it with everything he had and holding it there."Not this time. You're not winning this time," Dean spat out loud.

"Dean?" Tom reached out blindly. "Dean?" His hand found Dean's shoulder and he grabbed on tightly. "Man, is it ever dark in here."

Dean let his instinct guide his hand into the velvet bag. The orb was smooth and cool to his touch and when he closed his hand around it a tingling sensation tickled the surface of his palm. This felt right. A pleasant sensation warmed his whole body as he pulled the orb from the bag. He opened his hand. The orb was radiant. Rays of soft light, like the soft glowing light of moonbeams on a clear night, emanated from the orb, gently reaching into the recesses of the darkness before them, chasing away the inky black shadows. Revealed before them was a large tunnel. The walls of the tunnel were wet and oddly shaped with large ruts from ceiling to floor. Obviously the continual, steady paths of water had left their marks throughout the endless years. They gleamed silver in the glow of the orb and every once in awhile a bead of water would capture the light and send a sparkling star of brilliance.

Dean glanced at Tom and smiled, "Let's go."

Tom snapped his jaw that up until this moment had been hanging open, shut, and followed his friend. The two boys stayed close together as they continued along the tunnel.

"How far do you think we will have to travel? I mean, how far do you think these tunnels run?" Tom questioned. He wasn't sure he liked the small space that passed for a tunnel. The walls seemed to close in somehow. "I mean, how long do you think we'll be down here?"

"I don't know. Underground tunnels and caverns can go for miles. Some are more difficult than others," he responded without thinking. "It's a good thing we have hoodies and track jackets on; we're going to need them. It can get really cold down here."

"How do you know that?" Tom questioned, pulling his hoodie closer around his neck. He was already starting to feel the damp chill.

Dean's mind stumbled into another memory. *"Come on son, don't be afraid. I'll keep you safe. Just remember, watch your step, make sure you always stay with me, and try not to touch anything with your bare hands."* Dean was unsure but knew his father would protect him, so he set off on his first cave adventure. It was a simple cave with only two rooms, but plenty of formations and curiosities for his father to teach him about. Stalagmites rose from the cave floor in towers of all sizes. Stalactites, formations of the opposite phenomenon, dripped from the roof of the cave. Both formed from water and the mineral deposits left behind. Dean had been fascinated.

The tunnel they were presently in didn't have any such formations but the walls were miles upon miles of flow stones and Dean found that equally as magnificent and beautiful.

Dean shrugged in response, not ready to share, his focus straight ahead at the end of the soft light of the orb. Needing a distraction, Dean questioned Tom. "So, tell me what you know about all of this. You must have grown up on this stuff."

"Yes, much of this is believed to be only folklore ....legend, you know? If memory serves me the Flaming Pearl represents spiritual perfection and the ancients believed the pearl symbolizes the most precious treasure of all in our culture – wisdom. Oh, it's also an amulet of luck."

Dean snorted. "Well that's a comfort isn't it?"

Tom continued, disregarding Dean's interruption. Now was as good a time as ever to break the news to Dean, "and Dean?" Tom hesitated.

"Yea?"

"When Mao said that each one of the objects you have to find is guarded by the *Spirit of the Way* what did you think he meant?." Tom questioned, knowing this was going to be unpleasant.

"I don't know, some kind of Karma thing, I guess. Why?" Dean stopped moving to turn around and face Tom.

Tom swallowed, his Adams apple bobbed. "Well, as far as I know, the *Spirit of the Way* is symbolized by only one thing." He looked hesitantly at his buddy.

Dean had a bad feeling. A really bad feeling.

"So? What is it ?"

Taking the plunge, and half expecting his voice to disappear again, Tom continued, "Dragons. Dragons symbolize the "spirit of the way", which brings eternal change. The dragon has always been the guardian of the Flaming Pearl in my culture. As far back in history as written script exists."

Dean stared at Tom for seconds that seemed to go on for minutes. "You're kidding, right? Fire breathing beasts with wings? That? That kind of dragon?"

"Yep."

"But Mao never said anything about dragons! Tell me you're kidding!" Dean yelled.

Tom could see a storm brewing in Dean's eyes and he knew what that meant. "Well, if it helps any, the fire of the dragon represents the soul's spark of light. And you are going after your soul," Tom offered.

Dean kicked the wall of the tunnel. "Somehow I doubt it!" he kicked it again, a familiar hot surge settling in his chest. "If I'd have known that..." he yelled into the air, "if I'd have known that....well at least I would have known!!" He finished lamely.

If you'd have known that you wouldn't have had the courage. Admit it, you don't have what it takes to do this.

At this point Dean couldn't stop The Whisperings, because they were speaking the truth. If he had known about the dragons he wouldn't have entered the tunnel. That was probably why Mao hadn't told him, he could see the weakness. Dragons!!! Dragons!! Real honest to God dragons!!

His anger propelled him forward. Anger, not only at Mao for not telling him the truth, but at himself, for his fear. Tom was watching him with those intense brown eyes of his, waiting for him to completely lose it. Like he usually did. Waiting for him to say all kinds of stupid, mean things to him that he would later have to apologize for.

He surprised himself by saying, "Your great-grandfather should have told me."

"I'm sure there was a reason why he didn't, Dean, " Tom defended Mao. "I tried and he took my voice. So I think there is a reason he didn't want you to know until you were already on the journey."

"He thought I'd bail, that's why. He thinks I'm weak," Dean stated matter-of-factly, moving down the tunnel.

You see? This is too much for you. Turn back, turn back. Tom will understand. The wizard lied to you....how can you trust him now?

Dean's resolve faltered. His steps slowed as he listened to the Whisperings. Encouraged, they continued.

That's it, why put yourself at risk? You know you won't succeed. Give up before someone gets hurt.

"Dean? What's wrong?" Tom nudged. "Dean?"

The orb became warmer, it's glow suddenly more intense. It was as though it were encouraging Dean to move forward. Casting light as far as it could to dispel the shadows creeping into Dean's mind.

"Go away," Dean pushed the Whisperings back. Not today, today I'm going forward. No matter what *you* say, as he once again squeezed the life out of the voice in his head.

"What? Where am I supposed to go?" Tom answered.

"Oh, not you. Never mind."

Tom thought to himself that Dean needed to get a handle on that talking-to-yourself thing he has going on.

Dean continued down the tunnel with meaningful steps meant to punctuate his thoughts. Somewhere in the darkness ahead he noticed something skitter across the path, a shadow within the shadows, something about the size of a big rat! Dean squinted his eyes, straining to see clearer.

"Did you see that?" he asked Tom.

"See what?" Tom answered, his voice a bit uneasy.

Well…. that answers that question. Dean kept moving. "Nothing, just jumpy I guess."

Soon they came to a dead end with one path leading right and one path leading left.

"Great, which way do we go?" Dean puzzled out loud.

And what was *that*! Definitely something with four legs. Definitely something with four legs, and a tail! Maybe it was a cave rat. A really big cave rat.

"What the heck was that!" Tom yelled, jumping back a few feet. "Dean! What was that?!"

Dean stepped back a step as well, still squinting in an attempt to catch a better look. It had two large round ears, a long snout that ended in a sharp point, and fur that stuck out in course tufts all over its body. It looked like someone had put too much hair gel on it and then went crazy pulling on its fur. It reminded Dean of his foster mom, the troll! That thought had Dean smiling. Yea, the troll. Right down to the beady yellow eyes! That's what she looked like after her one hundredth cigarette! By this time Dean was laughing out loud. Tom, of course, didn't get it and gave his buddy a 'have you lost your mind?' look. The ugly little animal turned its two beady, yellow eyes toward the boys and made a snarling sound. It was sitting in the middle of the left or right junction seemingly daring them to try to continue, its long rat-like tail curling toward the boys. Its large ears stood straight up and it seemed as if it was waiting for them to make a move.

"How do we get past that?" Tom worried aloud. "It looks like it might have really big teeth!"

Dean watched the little beast carefully. It didn't appear to be too aggressive. It seemed to be guarding the junction. Maybe it was there to make sure they went the right way. Maybe it was a good little beast. You know, one of those helpers that you see in the movies that keeps the hero on the right track.

"You know, it sure would be nice if someone could have given us a map or something. Isn't there usually a magic map that tells you which way to go in these 'quest' things? I mean seriously, how are we supposed to know which way to go?"

This just didn't have the ingredients of an adventure like the ones Dean always read under the covers at night.

Okay, here goes. Dean took a step forward. The beast sprung so fast towards Dean that he had no time to think. As it flew through the air, wings spread from its back and it flew straight for Dean's face. He ducked.

Not a cave rat! This guy's got wings!

Tom didn't duck. The strange beast landed dead center of Tom's face with its wings wrapped around his head and its legs spread on either side of his face. Tom shrieked in panic. His hands grabbed the fat belly of the beast and pulled but it seemed to be stuck. Its eyes were round like saucers and it made the strangest purring sound.

Tom was still shrieking.

Well! So much for the helper idea! Dean sprung forward hoping he could dislodge the fat little animal from Tom's face. The movie <u>Alien</u> came to mind when those things with all the legs attached themselves to a human face and all was lost. The human died! That thought gave new speed to Dean's hands.

Tom was still shrieking.

"Tom! Tom! Stop yelling man. I need to think!" Dean yelled.

"Phink! Phink! What do you need to phink aphout?!!" Tom's muffled remark shot out, disbelief in his tone. "Just get phis phing off me!"

"I'm trying, I'm trying!" Dean's hands carefully searched for a way to make the animal let go of Tom's face. It was still purring loudly and had closed its eyes. "Geez, Tom. I think it's gone to sleep!" Dean said in amazement.

"Ashleep! GET IT OFF!"

The sharp panic in Tom's voice had Dean quickly leaning closer to inspect just how attached the little guy was and it was at that precise moment that Dean realized something amazing. This was a special moment. The most special moment in the history of Dean and Tom's two year friendship. Something was happening between them that had never happened before. Usually it was Dean who was engulfed in fear and Tom being the voice of reason and problem solving the issue. Usually it was Dean who was in trouble and Tom was the one helping him out. Usually it was Dean's heart that was racing like a frightened rabbit. Dean's pupils that were dilated. Dean's palms that were sweaty. Dean's brain ready to explode with frustration. But not today. Not this time. This time it was Tom. Dean took an instant to marvel at this wonder. Just an instant, mind you, because in the middle of that instant Tom screamed again, "GET IT OFF!!!"

Dean was galvanized into action. Tom had always come through for Dean, always, without exception. Dean was going to do the same for Tom.

The purring sound became louder and louder. The creature's eyes were shut and it appeared to be sleeping. Dean leaned closer and tried to pry the wings off the sides of Tom's face.

Tom's sense of panic was rising and he could feel the hair from the furry little animal sticking up his nose. He blew air out of his nose heavily in an attempt to dislodge the hair, but the action only made the hair move consequently tickling the inside of his nose even more. He snorted again. The effect worsened again. Without any notice, Tom sneezed so forcefully that the eyes of the round eared beast popped open with a start and it screeched as it popped off Tom's face and flew straight for Dean.

"Oh, no you don't!" Dean shouted as he ducked to one side and swung his arm out to ward off any other landing attempts. He wasn't going to have that thing on his face! The winged creature flew toward the tunnel junction and just before it hit the wall veered off to the right and away from the boys.

"Well! I know which way I'm going! "Tom stated loudly as he covered his face with his hands and ran down the tunnel.... to the left!

And into the dark.

"Dean!" Tom yelled out, stopping suddenly.

"Right behind you!" Dean answered as he pulled the orb out of the bag hanging from his shoulder. It glowed with warmth, dispelling the gloom. "Let's go," Dean said softly as he brushed by his buddy to take the lead.

The two boys followed the winding tunnel uphill and down, this way and that, for what seemed like forever. Tom was still trying hard to shake the hebee jebees he experienced with that fat little animal attached to his face. He could still feel its furry little belly over his nose and its smooth paper thin wings wrapped around his head. Its little feet had sharp little claws that scratched his face when it first clung onto his cheeks. His hand came up to touch the scratches for the hundredth time in memory of the experience.

"You okay?" Dean asked for the tenth time.

Tom just nodded 'yes' and kept moving. After considerable time, exactly how much neither boy could know, as time seemed to move at a different pace in the tunnels, Dean and Tom noticed something different. The floor of the tunnel was becoming more uneven and they were obviously going uphill. Dean's legs were beginning to tire and his breathing was faster. The incline was gradual but nonetheless there. Within a half hour, the two boys were climbing over rocks and needing to use their hands to steady themselves as they made their way up a hill that was narrowing quickly to a small opening that appeared to be the end of the tunnel. A task made more difficult for Dean while holding the orb for light. Dean randomly thought it would be great if he had one of those caver's helmets with the mounted headlight, that way his hands would be free. Dean used to put his dad's on his head and hide under the covers to read after lights out. Once his dad caught him and laughed at how silly he looked. His dad promised that when he got old enough he would take him caving and show him the ropes. And he did. The year Dean turned eight his dad took him to his very first cave.

"Almost there. Wow, what a climb!" Tom puffed.

As they approached the small opening they concentrated on their footing. Loose rocks and uneven ground was making the climb dangerous. Dean got to the opening first. He poked his head through, relieved to find another chamber. It was wide with a smooth floor and some kind of light radiating into it. Dean tucked the orb into his pouch. Orange and gold shadows danced upon the walls. Both boys clamored into the new tunnel and started toward the light source. As they got closer the opening widened and the colors became brighter, more vibrant. The dance became a little wilder.

"There must be something up ahead. See how the colors dance?" Tom whispered.

Dean's shoulders tightened in apprehension. The two boys had traversed the dangerous hill in mutual silence partially because Dean knew Tom was still upset, but also because complete concentration meant the difference between making the hill or finding yourself tumbling down the jagged slope. Either way the lack of conversation had left Dean alone with his thoughts to wage a mighty war. He'd run through all the reasons why he would never be able to do what was needed and then countered them with every reason why he could. He hadn't been able to help Tom when he needed it, had he? He was losing the battle. The weight of not believing in himself added an almost unbearable heaviness to his steps. Dean stopped. His blue eyes were soft and silently pleading.

Tom shook his head. "You must go on. You have nothing to lose."

Dean ran his hand through his curly blond hair to scratch the back of his head. Then he reached into the pouch and touched the orb. His instincts had been right about the glowing sphere, maybe they would help him now as well.

Blue eyes met brown ones. "You think I'm a coward, don't you?"

"I know you're *not* a coward," Tom replied, holding Dean's gaze firmly.

The weight lessened somewhat.

"I know you can do this," Tom added, a certainty in his eyes, and memories of his friend, trying desperately to help him only hours before, fresh in his mind.

The weight lessened even more.

"I'm right behind you, all the way," Tom continued.

The weight became bearable. Dean stepped forward.

The massive cavern spread itself grandly before them. The ceiling was magnificent in height. Long stalagmites hung throughout the chamber, each one aglow with the orange and gold light that danced wildly throughout the massive cavern. The hypnotic dance of color splashed its way into nooks and crannies, invading every space of the uneven, rutted walls of this magnificent underground room.

Dean and Tom stood stunned with awe. Captured by the sheer size of the formidable space, they remained mesmerized as they watched the poetry of motion before them.

It was Tom who noticed the flames first. He backed up a step. Or two. The entire base of the cavern was a sea of flames. Wild flames flickered and spewed. Flames as high as a house danced across the water, rising to lick the walls of the cave, and then receding only to rise even higher the next time. The heat of the room punched through the boy's awe, and Dean noticed sweat rivulets running down the middle of his back and swiped the wetness off his forehead before it could sting his eyes.

"Angry," Dean thought. "The flames look angry. The flames looked the way Dean sometimes felt. The anger inside him acted very much like the flames down below. Spewing forth their heat and then withdrawing, only to end up spewing even further the next time. As if they had no control and as they burned they gathered more heat until they became self sustaining. Dean thought about his parents and felt that burn, that rage sitting inside him, feeding itself. Dean's rage had become self sustaining long ago. He had let it feed and burn uncontrolled for a long time now. He was tired of his anger. Tired of the energy it took to sustain his flame. God, he missed his parents. "Why did you leave me?" he cried out loud.

"Dean? Are you all right?"

Tom couldn't believe his eyes. Dean stood next to him with tears running down his face. Not sweat… tears. Dean. The guy who showed about as much emotion as a sheet of metal. Dean. The guy with cast iron armor around his feelings. Standing there, crying.

"Why did you leave me?" he screamed out into the cavern. His cry echoed through the hollow air.

"Who? Who left you Dean?" Tom asked.

"My parents! Mom and Dad! They left me!"

Confused, Tom questioned," Dean, your mom and dad died, didn't they?"

"YES! They left me. Left me here with no one. NO ONE! No family, no one who cared a damn bit about what happened to me. I hate them for leaving me behind!" Dean sobbed. "I wish I had gone that night, to the show. Maybe things would have turned out differently. Maybe they wouldn't have died. They asked me if I wanted to go and I said no. I didn't want to hang with my parents. I thought they were old and boring. I wanted to hang with my friends."

Dean looked out into the cavern and yelled," I hate myself for not going and I hate them for dying!" The pain clenched his heart and tightened until he thought it would stop beating. He raged and screamed into the wild light until he felt something touch his shoulder. Gently, but insistently. It was Tom.

"Dean, Dean," Tom turned him to face his dark eyed friend. "Dean, stop. I know it must be so hard for you. I can't even imagine what I would do if my parents were killed. Your parents didn't mean to leave you behind. No one ever thinks they're going to die. They loved you. They loved you more than you'll probably ever know."

Dean stood before Tom with tear stained cheeks, clutching each word Tom was saying like a lifeline. He could feel himself being pulled to safety with every word. "You didn't do anything wrong, Dean. You did what kids do. It just turned out really awful for you. Who could have known? I'm so sorry you don't have any family. But, I can be your family. My family can be your family. Let us be your family. Not that TROLL you live with. She'll never be your family. You've got me. Right?"

Dean's heart hurt. But something was different. With each word Dean yelled, sobbed and wrenched from his gut it was as if the pain was shrinking. Becoming smaller, not totally going away, but somehow less oppressive. And someone did care. Tom cared. Maybe he did belong somewhere. Shrinking pain. Dean wondered briefly if he could manage to turn his pain into a tiny little shriveled grain of sand someday, or maybe more realistically, a small pea. "Right," Dean whispered, "I have you."

The flames surged upwards and hissed out to Dean. *You don't have the strength. Can't stand the heat. Go home now, before you get burned. Come to us and we'll scorch your heart, burn out that pain. Just step into the flame.* Dean shook the words from his head. Shut up. I'm not listening to you. He spun around and leaned out the entrance to the tunnel. His blue eyes pierced the flame, looking for what he knew stood engulfed.

Eternal Change.

Did Eternal Change have to be so immense? As Dean watched with a slack jaw the shimmering blue beast spread its wings and threw back its head to spew flames into the air hundreds of feet to the cavern ceiling. The heat from the blast punched through the air and slammed Dean and Tom back a step. The dragon turned its elegant head towards the boys and found Dean's eyes with its own. Sparkling white, shimmering from within, the eyes challenged Dean to try. Try to take the Pearl that rested within its claws. The dragon beat its wings, creating a thunderous sound and pushing the heat toward the boys once again. Its roar pierced the air, ending with an ear shattering scream as its spiked tail snapped and curled. The boys covered their ears. Its cool, sparkling eyes reflected the flames licking their way up the wall of the cavern. The Flaming Pearl, encased in blue flame, was cradled within the palm of the beast's paw.

"I knew it wouldn't be easy, but......." Dean left the remark hanging.

"Great-grandfather did warn us, but I never dreamed...." Tom's voice faded away.

Dean's mind frantically searched for the courage to do this task. This was not an easy thing because his courage was deeply buried amongst his fears. At this point fear was racing through Dean at breakneck speed, leaving an electrical surge in its wake, charging every nerve ending in his body. His courage seemed a long ways off. It was like finding pearls in the sand. A daunting task. One that seems unlikely to complete. As Dean looked out at the task before him he wondered how he could possibly do this thing.

One step at a time, Dean. Whenever anything seems too big to tackle you have to break it into small pieces. Don't look at the whole thing, but a little bit at a time. Then, before you know it, you've done what you need. Right, son?

Remembering his father's words, Dean slowly plucked one pearl and then another until he had them all collected and stored away. Only one pearl left to collect.

Taking a deep breath he opened the velvet bag. Inside were the two charms. Which one should he use? The Living Bean? The Iyc Crystal? What if he used the wrong one?

"Dean," Tom interrupted his thoughts, "which one are you going to use?"

"I don't know," Dean admitted.

"Great-grandfather said the Living Bean becomes your thoughts. Why don't you think of taming the dragon, putting out the flames, and toss it?" Tom offered.

"Oh of course, that's all hey?" Dean scowled. Easy for Tom. He didn't have to war with the options. His voice held disdain when he continued, "Gee Tom, why don't *you* pick? Why don't *you* go down and TAME the beast? Like seriously, are you for real?"

"Sorry," Tom offered. "I guess that did sound a little simplistic."

Tom remained quiet while he waited for Dean to decide which object he was going to use.

Dean still wasn't sure. He hesitated, then said, "I'll try the Living Bean."

He tossed the bean into the flames. It sprouted while in the air and sent out green shoots that instantly turned into flames. It grew and grew, the tendrils reaching everywhere. The flames grew brighter and hotter. Grotesque faces formed within the flickering flames and the hot tendrils curled and twirled, reaching out to grab the two boys. Evil laughter echoed in the cavern and the red glowing eyes of each beast burned brightly. One tendril of flame curled under the magnificent dragon and picked it up. The dragon spewed hot fire and stretched out its enormous wings as the curl of flame danced it around the cavern, moving closer and closer to where the two boys stood.

Tom and Dean jumped back and scrambled to the mouth of the tunnel, each step meant to avoid the scorching touch of the flames licking their way through the air. A deafening roar resounded through the cavern ending in a high pitched screech. Sinister laughter mocked the escaping boys.

Once well inside the tunnel, the boys collapsed to the floor gasping in fear. Dean coughed and sputtered, "That .....that's what I thought?! It....it," Dean coughed again, "must be. I was afraid the," another gagging cough, "whole thing would come after us ... but that?!"

Suddenly the bean rocketed across the cavern and shot into the tunnel, spewed out like some grotesque tasting food. It landed next to Dean, scorched and steaming with heat.

"You must control your fears and thoughts better!"

"Something tells me I picked the wrong charm!" Dean choked.

"No!" Tom burst out. "You just have to control your emotions. Try again."

Dean hesitated a moment. Mao's last words drifted into Dean's mind. "Your path may not always be obvious but it is always before you. The fire of the heart turns to ice when unused. To find...."

The fire of the heart! Ice! With a smile he turned to the mouth of the cave. The evil laughter still echoed loudly and the grotesque flames grew and flickered as before. The dragon stood proud and beat its wings. Dean took the Iyc Crystal from the velvet bag, walked to the edge of the tunnel, and hurled it into the sea of flames.

Tom reached out to stop him, but his hand grasped only air. He was too late.

The Iyc Crystal tumbled through the flames, magically transforming each tendril, each flicker, each dancing flame into sparkling blue crystal, before finally landing in the water. A splash of cobalt crystallized, and slowly, fingers of ice spread and quickly wove a solid shiny mass. The entire cavern had been turned into an icy, iridescent wonderland. Stalactites and stalagmites coated in frost glistened and sparkled. Light shimmered from every crystal, every flake, creating brilliant light. The dragon was frozen, with its scaly body reared up on its hind legs, wings spread in mid flight, and the clawed limb that held the Flaming Pearl outstretched, as if offering the magical sphere.

Dean looked triumphant. Tom slapped his hands together.

Dean laughed. "I was right. Can you believe that?"

"I always believe what is before my eyes. Boy, am I ever glad you didn't listen to me again!"

Dean smiled, and started toward the dragon. It was like one of those movies where an evil beast turns to stone before your eyes. The bright eyes of the dragon twinkled and sent sparks of light toward Dean, beckoning. He ventured onto the ice slowly, then realized he had nothing to fear. He had passed the test. He wove his way through the sharp, jagged mountains of iridescent ice shards toward the dragon. The crystal beneath his feet sparkled and glinted from within. Maybe the crystal does hold the secrets of the world, Dean mused.

So this is what Eternal Change looks like. The dragon, a perfect likeness of the ones riding Mao's lapels, towered, frozen, with an outstretched arm. In its long claws it held the Flaming Pearl. Blue and silver flames rippled over the surface. Its eyes were two huge diamonds, sparkling sharply in the crisp light. Shards of intense light ricocheted around the room. The shards moved with lightning speed, increasing in intensity. There was an energy in the air. An energy that was building in volume. Dean knew he had to move fast. Time was running out. The Dragon was so large that Dean had to climb upon its knee, swing up onto the arm and inch out toward the claws. The Pearl was so big! How could he possibly carry that? He reached the Pearl, leaned over to remove it from its resting place and was amazed at the weight of it. It weighed more than the neighbor, Mrs. Nettle's, dog! Dean turned himself around and started inching his way back when he noticed something. The Pearl was shrinking! The flames were cool to touch and the Pearl was shrinking! By the time Dean reached the belly of the Dragon the pearl was the size of a jawbreaker! He tucked it into his velvet pouch. Smugly he thought, "*I have spiritual perfection in the bag.*"

"Hurry up, Dean! Something is happening!" Tom yelled from below.

Dean slid down the shiny, blue, belly, landing at the feet of the huge statue. "Wow! What a ride!" he whooped. He looked up. The Dragon's wings were outstretched, frozen in flight, and for a moment Dean feared it coming to life too soon, grabbing him in its huge claws and flying away with him, leaving him no way to regain his reflection. The air cracked and snapped. Sensing that something was about to happen, he looked around for a way out.

"DEAN!!! LET'S GO!" Tom hollered.

"Over here! I see another tunnel!" Dean gestured.

The crystals and ice cracked and heaved as the boys ran towards the dark mouth of another tunnel. Towers of crystal toppled and shattered to the base of the cavern. The boys dove into the tunnel just before a flash of light exploded, the energy sending Dean and Tom flying through the air.

Chapter 5

The boys landed just inside the tunnel with a loud
CRACK as their heads met, knocking them both unconscious.

*"Dean, Dean, come look at this! This is called CaveBacon.
Look what happens when I shine the light behind it!"*

*Dean scrambled over the loose rocks to where his dad was
standing. Wow, it really did look like bacon! His dad was so excited as
he explained how it was formed. The bacon curled and twisted its way
across the wall of the cave for several feet.*

*"Son, this is a great find. You don't see Cave Bacon
everywhere you go. Indeed, this is special."*

*Dean was once again fascinated with all the unusual rock
formations and weird shapes clinging to the roof of this small cave.
"Dad, what are those?" Dean asked as he pointed to the roof.*

"Those? Well son, those are called Soda Straws."

*"I can see why. That's exactly what they look like. The straws
mom buys are exactly like that, except they have red stripes,"
Dean agreed with a chuckle. He reached out to touch one but
his father's shout stopped his hand mid air.*

"Dean! No! Remember, don't touch anything."

*"Sorry Dad, I forgot," Dean apologized, belatedly
remembering his father's explanation about how the oil off the human
hand coats the limestone, creating a void where the water won't run,
thus halting the growth of the formation. He quickly put his hand
down and was content to stretch up on his tiptoes to get a better look
at the hundreds of Soda Straws on the ceiling of the cave. This was the
second time Dean's dad had taken him caving since he'd turned eight.
Each time Dean learned more about the sport and was able to go*

urther into the cave. His dad told him he was proving himself to be a
very responsible caver and Dean smiled with pride.

Dean was still smiling when he awoke from his dream. He stirred and immediately raised his hand to the whopper bump on the side of his head.

"Ahhh!" he moaned loudly. Gingerly touching the area around his goose egg, he checked for blood.

Tom stirred slowly, also bringing his hand up to the egg on his head and moaning, "Ohhhh, what the.....?"

Rolling onto their backs the two boys lay there trying to find their bearings. Both felt dizzy and somewhat nauseated.

"I knew you were hard-headed. I feel like I ran into a cement wall," Tom complained while holding his head.

"Well I don't feel like I ran into a marshmallow, that's for sure. So your skull must be pretty thick too," Dean grunted back as he attempted to sit up. The walls of the tunnel swayed and small black dots danced before his eyes. His stomach pitched and rolled. With an I'm-gonna-be-sick groan Dean fell back to the ground. "I think I need to lay here for awhile."

The two boys lay in silence, each one trying to quiet their traitorous stomachs in their own way.

"My dad was a caver," Dean said, his eyes closed.

"What?"

"You asked me how I knew about caves."

"Oh, right."

"My dad was a caver," Dean repeated.

"What's a caver?"

"Someone who explores different caves and caverns. Sometimes caverns go deep inside the mountains but sometimes they are underground where you would never expect them. Cavers use harnesses and ropes to propel down the walls and into large networks of underground rooms. My dad started teaching me how to cave when I was eight. I was just getting to the age where I would have been able to learn how to use ropes, grips and harnesses.

"And then your dad died."

Dean squeezed back the pain. "Yea."

"I'm sorry." The words seemed too small but they were all Tom had to offer.

"My dad was a high school teacher. My mom was a geologist. They met when my dad went to the office where she worked looking for maps." Dean heard the story of their whirlwind romance many times. As a young boy he would groan and roll his eyes, pretending to die from the mush of it all. Now he would give anything just to hear their voices once again.

"Who do you look like?"

"My dad. But my mom always said I had her smile." Dean's mouth turned up at the corners in the merest hint of the smile he was picturing on his mother's face. For some reason it didn't bring the familiar pain. Instead a gentle sigh escaped and Dean allowed the image of his mother to hover before him.

You can do this son. We have faith in you. Don't despair. Difficult times like these are the true measure of a person. Anyone can be gracious during the good times, but only truly strong and honorable people extend their graciousness during the worst of times. You are a good person, Dean. You have a good heart. We trust you will make the right decision.

His mother's words washed over him, warming his soul, strengthening his resolve and easing his pain.

"Mom?" Dean reached out, believing if he wanted it bad enough he could touch the image before his eyes. But his hands found only air. And the image of his mom faded to nothing. As if it had never been, although the warmth remained.

"So what you're telling me is that you have a girly smile?" Tom teased, wanting to ease the pain in his friend's voice. "Always figured you were too cute."

Dean rolled over onto his stomach, hoping it and his head wouldn't rebel. He punched his smiling friend in the arm. "Watch it buddy. I may have to hurt you," he warned playfully.

"Oh yea, you and whose army?" Tom rolled over and pushed up to his hands and knees.

Dean reached out and pushed him before he could steady himself. Tom toppled onto his side. And the wrestling match was on, goose bumps and uneasy stomachs forgotten.

Being taller and about twenty pounds heavier Dean had Tom yelling UNCLE after only a few strategic flips and holds. They both collapsed once again, breathing heavily, but feeling much better.

"So, now what?" Tom asked, still trying to catch his breath.

Dean glanced into the tunnel, seeing only the black void he'd become familiar with. His hand was drawn to the velvet pouch at his side. "We move ahead."

The orb's gentle light banished the darkness once again and the boys started down the tunnel. This one was much smaller than the others, smaller and much wetter. The two friends found themselves side stepping puddles of water and listening to the constant trickling and plunking of droplets. Dean found the familiar music a very calming symphony, one that extended itself into the crevices of Dean's being and left its influence. It reminded him of the old wizard. Somehow Dean knew the old man would find peace and wisdom in the water's music. Letting go and trusting where one will land, that sort of thing.

In the course of jumping and shuffling through the tunnel, Tom ended up in the lead and although Dean was experiencing a calming effect as he made his way down the tunnel Tom wasn't. In fact, Tom was experiencing just the opposite feeling and soon he would wish that he hadn't earned the lead. Very soon. The tunnel quickly began shrinking in size.

"The tunnel's definitely getting smaller," Tom mumbled.

"What?"

"I said, the tunnel's definitely getting smaller," Tom repeated with great emphasis.

"So, bend over a bit," Dean returned, missing the troubled tone in Tom's voice.

Soon the tunnel was small enough the boys had to crawl to continue.

"Dean, this is ridiculous. We can't keep going. Maybe we took the wrong tunnel," Tom complained. Beads of sweat were forming on his brow and his breath was short, as if he were doing something strenuous.

Dean frowned. The air in the tunnel was cool and damp and they weren't going uphill, so what was wrong with Tom? "There was only one way out, remember?"

"Maybe we missed one. Maybe the other tunnel was hidden. Maybe this way will get us in trouble. Maybe we'll die!" Tom yelled the last three words as he twisted his body and looked back.

Dean wasn't quite sure what to say to that. "Die? From what? Crawling on our hands and knees? What's wrong with you?"

Tom took a deep breath. "Nothing," he snapped" Let's just get to the end of this blasted tunnel!'

Soon the boys were crawling on their bellies like a pair of lizards. Tom stopped. His feet started banging up and down. Dean dodged a foot to the face. "Hey! I'm back here, remember?"

"I'm not going any further!' Tom yelled, panic in his voice.

"What? Why not? We're probably almost there."

"No! No further! It's just getting smaller and smaller. I refuse to go any further!" Fear drove Tom's voice higher in pitch.

"But..."

"No buts, Dean! I mean it! FORGET IT! Over my dead body!!!!" Tom screamed in pitches high enough to make Dean cover his ears.

Dean got another foot in the face as Tom started backing up, moving away from the ever shrinking walls of the tunnel ahead.

"Whoa!"

"Get out of my way Dean. GET OUT OFMY WAY!"

"Okay, okay.....we'll go back Tom, but you've got to calm down. I can only back up so fast. You keep kicking me."

Tom was in the firm grip of panic but managed to explain, "I can't stand being this closed in. I feel like I'm smothering! I can't breathe. I want to scream!"

"Okay, okay, I know you're panicked, but be realistic Tom. I can only back up so fast. It sounds like you have claustrophobia," Dean tried to reason.

"REALLY....what was your first clue?" Tom sneered sarcastically.

Dean ignored the comment and continued in the same calm but firm tone. "I heard that if you close your eyes tight and imagine you're in a huge field, you know, a wide open space, the sun is shining, the wind is blowing, if you imagine you are there instead, it will help the panic you're feeling. Keep moving and picture that, okay?"

"Easy for you to say," Tom's voice wasn't so sharp, the edge dulled with hope. It seemed he liked the idea, which totally amazed Dean because he was making up every single word.

Dean could sense Tom's need for a chance out of this. He continued, "Green grass swaying in the breeze, fluffy white clouds drifting through the sky. The birds are singing, you can see the mountains way off in the distance..."

Tom shuffled backwards to the sound of Dean's voice spouting every descriptive, flowery sentence he could think of to keep him going.

Boy would Mr. Statler be proud of me! He always said my English stories lacked imagination!

"You're playing tag, running free with Scruffy, your trusty sheepdog," Dean added for effect. He was really getting into this.

Soon the tunnel widened enough for them to switch to crawling on all fours. Relief washed over Tom.

"The breeze is blowing....."

"Okay, okay! That's good Dean. I don't feel so....so...."

"Afraid?" Dean finished.

"I wasn't afraid," Tom defended. "I just don't like small spaces."

"Oh, yea, right. Don't like small spaces. I get it," Dean patronized his buddy.

Tom turned and plunked himself down to a sitting position. He flicked Dean on the head. "Hey, let up okay? I can't explain it, I can't control this crazy panic that takes hold of me and I feel like I'll go crazy if I don't get out. It's not a feeling I ever want to feel again. So let up."

"Sorry." Dean had never seen Tom so unsure of himself. It was weird. But, nobody's perfect, right? Even guys like Tom have things that make them vulnerable. This was another rare moment in their friendship.

The two boys stood before the only other tunnel leading out of the Sea of Flames. They could feel the heat on their backs and hear the roar of the dragon as they stared into yet another dark void.

"Too bad we missed this earlier," Tom grumbled.

Dean shot him a quick look filled with humor and repressed laughter. "It's okay, Tom. Your secret is safe with me."

Tom sneered and snorted, "Yea right. Like you're not going to tell anyone. I can see it now. Ooooh, Tom's afraid of small spaces. What's the matter Tom? Then they'll shove me in a locker just to see me lose it," Tom voiced his fears.

Offended, Dean's voice became short and gruff. "Hey! I said I wouldn't tell. And I won't. You think I don't know what it's like to be afraid. Seriously man, I've got your back." He paused, then continued, "Stop insulting me, will ya. I think I'm a better friend that that."

"Sorry, geez, I sure am jumpy, hey. I think I just need to take a break," Tom apologized "That whole thing back there wore me out." He really did feel tired, like the energy was sucked out of him. "Can we just stop and rest for a bit?" As he dropped down to sit on the edge of the tunnel entrance Tom remembered the energy bar and candy in his pocket. "Hey! Dean! Look what I found!" He pulled them out and dangled them as if offering a tantalizing treat.

"I can do you one better!" Dean boasted, pulling out four packages of peanuts and a granola bar.

"I forgot about your obsession with peanuts!" Tom laughed. "But I'm glad of it now!"

They put all the food in a pile on the ground in front of them in a pile and sorted through, trying to decide how to ration their supplies.

"How long do you think?" Tom left the question hanging, knowing that Dean couldn't know the answer any more than he did. He just couldn't resist asking it. Dean appeared to be so focused and in general good spirits that Tom was confused because he was feeling just the opposite. He was feeling edgy, unsettled and very unsure of himself. Not a feeling he was accustomed to. Usually Tom was steady as a rock. He was still somewhat shaky from the shrinking tunnel experience. A weakness had settled in his limbs; he needed rest.

"Okay, so let's eat only enough to keep us going. I can't seem to track time down here but I think we are definitely due for a snack. How about we split one package of peanuts and each have a half a granola bar?" Dean suggested.

Tom nodded in agreement. "Sounds good."

Dean watched the Sea of Flames perform their fiery dance and let his eyes survey the cathedral sized room. He noticed the deposits of minerals around the outside of the pool. "Rimstone Dams," he said out loud, not to anyone in particular.

"What?'

"Rimstone Dams," he repeated. "That's what those deposits are around the outer edges of the main pool." They're like small bodies of water, like tide pools, you know, when the water goes out it leaves behind these cool pockets of water where starfish, crabs and such live. That's how I think of Rimstone Dams. Only without the starfish," Dean grinned.

"Speaking of water, we need to drink. Do you think this water is clean enough to drink?"

"I don't know for sure. I know there are micro-organisms in the water, but there is in any. Will it hurt us? Who knows. I do know we have to stay hydrated though." Dean looked around at the outer walls. "I think the water coming down the cavern walls would be cleaner."

So they drank from the trickling streams, cupping their hands to catch small pools and then slurping the mineral water from their palms.

"How many caves did your dad take you to?" Tom wanted to know more about Dean's family but knew he had to be careful about how he asked his questions. Dean seemed to want to talk about his dad, wanted to share those experiences he and his father had had. Really, in the two years he'd known Dean he'd never found out any details about his family. And yet, Dean knew everything about his. Dean knew that Tom's parents were Canadian born Chinese. That his dad worked at a computer technology company called No Brainer. His mother worked with Immigrant Services, helping people who have immigrated to Canada find work, learn English and settle into the community. He knew Tom's sister, Anna, a 10-year-old who had a crush on her brother's best friend. He also knew that sometimes Tom's parents golfed on Sundays, leaving him to babysit his little sister. That's when Tom would bring Anna along if he and Dean had plans. Sometimes they took Anna to the movies, bowling or just to hang out at the park. Dean knew Tom was a good brother. Dean knew that the house Tom lived in had a modern oriental flair but was not traditional like the restaurants. Tom was raised with the air of oriental wisdom and learned to speak the language fluently. His mother demanded no less. Dean knew all these things about Tom's life but had guarded his own vehemently. Never sharing anything about his life prior to the day Tom met him at John's. So he repeated his question. "How many caves did your dad take you to?"

"Six," Dean answered. "It wasn't always just dad and me. Mom came with us a couple of times. We would always make sure there was a cavern somewhere close by on our holidays. Mom liked to hike too."

"Do you remember which ones?"

"Every single detail." His voice was soft with emotion. "Carlsbad Caves was the first famous one we went to. Some of the others were great caves to learn in but not on a list of 'gotta see' caves. One year we went to Texas and got to see two really cool caves. Inner Space Cave and Natural Bridge Caverns. The one I really wanted to see was the Lost Sea. Apparently it is the largest underground lake in the world. I can't remember where it is but it was found by a thirteen- year- old boy. Divers can't find a bottom to it. Creepy, hey? Who knows what's under the surface. The cavern is so big that the light has nothing to bounce off of so it is lost. Pitch black darkness with a pinprick of light. Too cool. One day maybe I'll go there," he ended with a whisper.

"I'd like to go too," Tom added. "But for now I guess we have a tunnel to travel."

Dean shook off the sadness creeping into his heart. "Right, let's go."

Refreshed and rested they put away the rest of their supplies, brushed themselves off and turned to face the tunnel. Dean's hand found the orb. It was so natural, so...right, the way it fit his hand, warmed his palm. He couldn't remember a time when he's felt so, what was the word? So at peace with himself? Yes, that but more. He felt a sense of inner power, a foreign feeling, until now.

Chapter 6

Another tunnel. This one was much roomier than the last but with the same rutted walls slick with mineral water, the same damp smell, the same wandering path. Then Dean looked up.

And stopped.

The whole ceiling was covered in knob-like clusters, hundreds of them.

"Tom, look up!"

"Wow, what are they?"

"Cave popcorn."

"Cave what? Did you say popcorn?"

"Yea. It's actually, one of the most common formations, but I think it's cool anyway."

"Why do they name everything after food? Cave bacon, cave popcorn, soda straws. It's making me hungry," Tom complained.

Dean laughed. "I don't know. I never thought of that, but you're right."

Dean was still chuckling over his friend's astute observation when he stopped suddenly. A rush of sound was making its way toward them.

"Shhhh, what is that?"

Tom angled his head, trying to identify the approaching sound. Unable to pinpoint it exactly, he nudged Dean. "What is that?"

"I asked first."

Then suddenly, recognizing the frantic flapping, Dean yelled out, "Get down!" As he threw himself to the floor of the tunnel, he grabbed Tom's arm and pulled him down with him. Just as they hit the floor the wild rush of flapping wings came roaring over their heads. Hundreds of bats fluttered through the tunnel on a mad race toward some unknown destination.
"Stay down! And pull your hood up over your hair!"

But his warning came too late.

Tom wasn't as quick to hit the dirt, so to speak, and certainly not able to get his hoodie up! He felt the tug of little feet, tangled, and frantically pulling on Tom's somewhat long, jet black, oriental hair. Tom screamed like a girl, his arms flailing wildly, and shuffled from one side of the tunnel to the other on his knees. Blind fear removed all possibility of reason. His brown eyes were black pools of terror.

If Dean hadn't been so horrified for his friend he would have been rolling on the ground laughing. If he hadn't been so horrified...but he was, and frozen, for just a split second.

He looked up at the river of bats flapping wildly overhead and remembered the bats of Bracken Cave. Every summer night twenty million bats rush outside to feed on insects. It takes take up to three hours for all twenty million to emerge. Dean's dad took the family there when they were in Texas. The river of bats form a column so large that it shows up on radar screens and the wind created from their wings rustles the leaves on the nearby trees. Dean thought it was the coolest thing he'd ever seen. His mom wasn't too enthusiastic; she didn't like bats. She was afraid of them getting caught in her hair. He shook himself loose of the memory.

That's when he realized Tom was in trouble. He was screaming like a princess party girl, while a bat flapped frantically on his head, its small talons caught in his long ebony hair. Dean pulled Tom down between his legs and put a leg lock on Tom's waist. With no time to reason, and a madman squirming and flailing in his leg hold, Dean forced his mind to focus on the frightened, furry rodent flapping on the top of Tom's head. Fighting to concentrate solely on the feet, and disentangling them from the long strands of black hair, Dean tried not to listen to Tom's frenzied screams of terror. One last strand and...yes, it joined the horde on their journey through the tunnel. Dean quickly pulled Tom's hood up over his head and released him. The deafening *whoosh* tapered suddenly to silence, with only the odd remnant bat fluttering behind the horde, and a soft brushing of wings in the distance.

Tom was still screaming.

"Tom! Tom!" Dean yelled at his buddy. Without thinking, Dean punched him. Hard. Hard enough to break through the fog of terror that had closed its claws around Tom's mind.

"Hey! That hurt!" Tom accused, rubbing his shoulder and getting to his feet. "Thanks, I think."

"Anytime," Dean put his fists up in a fighter's stance. "You wanna go a round?" he joked.

"Wouldn't want to hurt you," Tom returned. "Holy crap, Dean. That was freakin' harsh man!"

"No kidding...man, that was kinda freaky. Bats are a bit creepy, hey?"

"Creepy? You are the master of understatements. Creepy? How about the worst experience of my life. How about so scared I think I peed myself," as he checked the front of his pants, fully expecting them to be wet.

Suddenly Dean couldn't contain himself. He burst out laughing. Gut laughter that had tears rolling down his face, his arms folded over his stomach as if in pain and delight dancing in those watery blue eyes. He couldn't help it. The thought of Tom peeing himself just left him with no option but to laugh. Besides, the moment needed some serious lightening.

"Oh, I'm so glad you think this is funny," Tom spat out, indignant to the core. "Some friggin friend you are."

That only made Dean laugh more. Nasty words just seemed bizarre when they were coming out of Tom's mouth.

Tom stood, staring in disbelief, as his friend continued to bruise his dignity. Then suddenly he burst out in his own fit of laughter. "Man, I must have looked insane! Let's get this done!"

The tunnel proved to be short. A connector from one room to another. The smell reached the boys before the entrance. A repugnant, musty smell, sharp to the senses.

"Okay, that's rank man." Tom's hand came up to his face, as if the gesture would somehow filter out the smell attacking his nostrils.

"Oh, you're not gonna like this," Dean warned.

"Why? What is that smell?"

"It's what they call guano. Bat poop."

"Bat poop? You're kidding, right?"

"Nope. All those bats have got to be roosting somewhere. And where there's a colony of bats, there's bat poop." As Dean reached the entrance to the cave he stopped, leaned out with the orb and said, "Lots and lots of bat poop."

"GREAT," Tom said with a tone that said he thought this was anything but great.

"Hey, just think At least the bats are out feeding. Which by the way, means it's past sundown. Anyway, with the bats out of the cave we can get through this room a lot easier," Dean pointed out.

"The room is filled with large piles of bat crap!"

Dean ignored the sarcasm dripping from the last word.

"We'll have to stick to the edges of the cave. There's less guano there," Dean directed, giving special emphasis to the word *guano*.

Unimpressed, Tom just grunted.

The orb glowed, sending its gentle moon rays to dispel the shadows. Instinctively, Dean looked toward the ceiling while holding the orb as high as he could. Quick laughter escaped followed by, "I don't believe this."

"NOW WHAT!" Tom's exasperated tone an accurate indication of how short tempered he was feeling.

"It's okay, Tom," Dean reassured. "It's just another formation on the roof of the cave, see?" Pointing upward, Dean directed Tom's gaze. "Guess what they're called?"

"Dean, I'm not up for twenty questions!"

Dean replied, humor still lacing his tone, "Carrot patch or the longer name is worm's eye view of a carrot patch."

"At this point I think I'd rather be Bugs Bunny looking at Elmer Fudd's carrot patch. Let's forget the worms. Okay?"

"Ahhh, what's up Doc?" Dean mimicked.

"Why does everything have to be so..." Tom's leg shot out as he felt something crawling inside his pant leg. "Creepy!" he finished. "Something's crawling up my leg!" he yelled.

Dean could feel something making its way up his leg also. He shook one, then the other. He lowered the orb. The ground was moving. Millions of black beetles crawled over one another in a blanket from one end of the cave to the other.

"They're feeding on the guano."

Dean gagged. He hated beetles. In the summer he was freaked out when those huge flying beetles came out, clicking as they flew and then sticking to your clothes. They creeped him out. When you stepped on one they made a huge CRUNCHING sound, and their guts would spill out. Dean's eyes searched the walls of the cave for the way out. He moved toward the end where darkness prevailed in the light of the orb. He grabbed Tom's jacket and tugged. "Come on! Let's get out of here!"

Chapter 7

A lake of blackness, dotted with uneven patches of stone, bubbled lazily, releasing steam and heat into the already too warm cavern. The two boys had already traveled around the outer rim of the cave, carefully picking their way over rocks and diligently avoiding the obviously hazardous edge of the bubbling mass. They passed what they assumed to be the shrinking tunnel's exit, a hole about a foot in diameter and six feet up the wall.

Obviously that wouldn't have worked.

Tom had simply offered his friend a raised eyebrow and a smug look.

The second tunnel they passed was what they agreed to call the *out* tunnel. And now they were right back where they'd started from. Black and red beetles crawled over their squashed mates on their way back home from the spot where Dean and Tom viciously swiped and shook them from their legs. They moved past the tunnel entrance, away from the left-over beetles, and sat down on the grouping of large boulders that offered the only spot up off the ground. Dean's arms rested on his knees. He laced his fingers and tapped his thumbs together as he looked out over the sticky goo bubbling in front of him. In the center, on a rocky knoll, a group of towering stones arranged themselves in a circle, jagged and formidable in size and presence. Dean sighed and looked a bit hopeless.

"This cave seems to be lacking *The Way*," Tom observed, nicknaming the missing dragon.

Understanding the joke, but also hoping it wasn't true, Dean returned with, "Maybe *The Way* can only be found once."

"Ya think? Except you would have to find *The Way* more than once to have eternal change, don't you think? It's not something that happens easily."

"Maybe there isn't anything to find here. Maybe we need to keep going. What do you think, Tom?"

Tom wasn't sure what to think. As much as he knew the fork lore of his culture, mystery and whispers shrouded the legend of the UnderWorld of Darkness leaving little but guesses about the details. His curiosity about the UnderWorld had never outweighed his childhood fear enough to question deeply. Shivers of the unknown stayed his tongue. Now he wished he had asked those questions. Maybe then he would be more help to his best friend. What he did know scared him, really scared him. He remembered once when he was about ten years old, before he'd met Dean, he'd done something stupid. Something that put a cloud of disappointment behind his father's otherwise, clear, brown eyes. Something that Tom tried hard to forget, because the memory of his act brought shame. For him, and for his family. It was then that his great grandfather had warned him.

"Young Tom, careful you must be, or find yourself searching in the Darkness. Those who enter may not return, the Darkness can swallow you whole. It takes not a part, but all that you are."

Tom had been frozen to the spot as his great-grandfather had spoken. Ancient mystery had swirled upon the air, giving energy and life to each molecule. Tom felt the charge racing over his body, making the hair on his arms and back of his neck stand up. At ten years old, Tom had learned the perils of losing oneself in the crowd, and had decided he never wanted to take that unknown journey. Something cloaked in darkness and always served up as a warning wasn't anything Tom wanted to experience. It wasn't that he was faint of heart or anything. No, Tom had as much courage as the next guy, some would say more. No, it wasn't a lack of guts, but a good dose of common sense, Tom liked to think. He just knew the difference between being brave and being stupid. Sitting next to Dean, once again he wished he had more insight to offer on the Underworld of Darkness. Lacking that ability, he offered up the insight he was able to share.

"It's tar."

Dean looked at his friend with skepticism. "Really, and you know that how?"

Tom shrugged. "Because I'm a genius, that's how," he replied.

Then he offered the truth. "I remember reading something years ago when I had to do this project about prehistoric animals. Sometimes big mammals like woolly mammoths or saber tooth cats would get stuck in the tar pits. Then they would die there and sink deeper and deeper. The tar would encase their bones and preserve them. Then forty thousand years later, we find them and put them together. Museums have actual woolly mammoths reconstructed. There's a place in Los Angeles, right in the center of the city, where the tar pit still exists and the museum is next to it. I kept bugging my parents to go there. La Brae. Yea, La Brae Tar Pit, that was the name."

Hands clasped, Dean glanced over at his friend. "Tar huh."

Tom nodded grimly. "Although, I don't know about the heat in here. It seems to me that a tar pit only releases gases. At least that's what I remember."

"Maybe this tar pit is sitting over a lava pool or something. Who knows, hey? Down here anything can happen."

His moment of distraction over, Dean continued, "So, now what?"

"Let's take another look."

"Look at what?"

"Around the outer edge. Maybe we missed something." Tom stood, swiped the dust off the seat of his jeans and put his hand out to Dean.

"Okay, we'll give it one more look." Dean took the offered hand and let Tom pull him off the rock. "What is it exactly we're looking for again?"

"I don't know. Anything that might be a clue, you know? Maybe Spiritual Perfection isn't so easy to find this time," Tom reasoned.

As they carefully walked around the pit, frustration edged its way into both of the boys. They were about to give up and move on to the next cavern when Dean noticed something on the stones that ran along the edge of the tar pit.
"Tom, look. What is that?" he pointed to the stone.

"It's a symbol. In the ancient language."

"What does it mean?"

"Well, it's in a dialect I'm not familiar with but I think it means *wisdom*."

"Wisdom? That's it? Wisdom?" exasperation strained Dean's voice. "What is that supposed to mean?"

"I don't kn...." Tom stopped mid word. "Look at that stone." He pointed to another stone a few meters away. "There is more than one stone with writings on it. Dean, it's an anagram. We just have to figure out what it says."

"Okay, but how do we know what order they go in. They are in a circle, no beginning and no end. And even if we do figure out what it says, what are we supposed to do with it?"

"Let's just get one thing done at a time. Okay? We need to find all the stones that have symbols on them." Tom bent his dark head over to read the script on the stone. "This one is *wisdom*. I'm sure of it."

Dean made his way to the second stone inscribed with ancient script. "What about this one, Tom?"

Tom looked at the symbol. "Gee Dean, I'm not sure about this one. I think it could be *speak*, but I'm not entirely sure.

"That makes sense though, Tom. Think about it. Speak wisdom. Makes sense, right?"

"Yea, it could. Let's find the others and then try to figure it out."

They continued around the tar pit, eyes scanning for another stone that could hold the key to Dean's future.

"There! There's another one! What does it say?" Dean asked, excitement making his voice unnaturally high.

Tom flashed him a grin. "Hey Dean, or should I say Dorothy? Your voice sounds like a girl!"

"Shut up! Whatever! What does it say?" Dean punched his friend in the shoulder.

"Okay, okay, just a minute. The script is familiar but somehow different. It isn't easy to read. Let's see. It looks like *seek*. Yea, I think it is seek, look for, or something like that."

"That's not good enough, Tom. We need to know exactly what it means, don't you think. Do we have any room for error here?"

"Okay, if I were to have to pick one, I'd say it is *seek*."

"You're sure?"

Tom frowned at his friend. "I'm going to ignore that question."

"Right, you weren't sure. God, Tom I have a feeling you need to be sure. So where does that leave me?" Dean worried aloud.

"One step at a time, remember?" Tom reminded his friend. "Look, I see another stone!"

"How many of these are there? We could be here a long time!"

"I know this one for sure. Totally for sure. *Courage*."

The search continued until both of the boys were positive that they had retrieved all the words from the stones. They inspected every rock at the edge of the tar pit, afraid they might miss something they needed. In the end they still had only four words. Courage, seek, wisdom and speak. And that's how they put them together.

"Courage seek, wisdom speak. It rhymes. Don't these kinds of things usually rhyme?" Dean offered.

"Your guess is as good as mine. It does make sense. To seek courage is honorable and to speak wisdom is honorable. Sounds pretty oriental to me," Tom joked. The serious part of him added, "It sounds like something my great- grandfather would say."

"So what *wisdom* am I supposed to speak?"

"Maybe just the word *wisdom*. Why else would these words be given to you?"

Dramatically, Dean stood on the edge of the tar pit and raised his arms, speaking the word *wisdom* in a loud, deep, commanding voice.

Nothing happened.

Tom snorted.

Dean blew a lock of blond hair off his forehead, turned around and walked back to the rock he'd been sitting on before they started looking for clues. He clasped his hands in his usual way, tapping his thumbs together. How did he get himself into this? And how was he going to find his way out?

The Longgu oracle is a spiritual script carved by the ancients on the shell of a tortoise. Heed the ancient language, it foresees your path and warns of the perils of darkness. Lose your way and all will be lost. There will be no return.

Mao's cryptic words echoed in Dean's mind. At the time they meant little to him but now they started to make sense. With each leg of the journey Dean realized how much of himself had been lost in the darkness. Dean was tired. The heat was sapping all his energy. Most of the caves he'd gone to with his father were damp and chilled. This was different. Sweat ran rivulets down his back, soaking his t-shirt. He took off his hoodie and laid it across his lap. Then he re-clasped his hands and continued to tap his thumbs together.

You're tired. Don't worry you can stop now and rest. This is too hard. Who needs the grief?

Dean gave the all too familiar voice a push.

You could die. Is that what you want? And what about Tom? You're putting him at risk. It'll be your fault if something happens to him. Just like before.

Dean wrapped an imaginary hand around the voice's throat. And squeezed. Doubt wound its way into Dean's heart. Out loud he ventured, "Tom? You know, it's not too late to turn back." Dean looked at the ground. "I mean you still could..." he wasn't sure how to finish. "I mean...you don't have to be here. You know? This isn't your problem," he finished quietly.

Tom sat quietly, thinking about the challenge in front of them. He understood that it was Dean's insecurity talking. He also understood that Dean had more to lose than he did. He even understood that some of what Dean was saying was born out of genuine concern for him.

But he was still offended. Highly offended. It showed in his voice. "Right, I guess I'll just truck myself back to where we came in and leave you to it." He shrugged, his nonchalance belying the indignation rising inside of him. "Really, it's not my problem."

Dean wasn't sure which part of Tom to believe. The scathing sarcasm in his voice or the devil may care body language.

See, he doesn't really want to be here. He doesn't care about your soul, why should you?

"That's right, I got myself into this. It's my problem, not yours." Dean's head rested in his hands. He squeezed his temples and sighed. How did I get here?

Because you're stupid, that's how. You have no backbone. You're nothing. Go back, before you get someone hurt.

Dean lifted his head and thought about what lay before him. He could feel Tom's eyes drilling into the side of his head. The force of his glare was so intense he swore he could feel the heat. He slowly turned to look at his friend and was shocked. Shocked to see such rage in eyes usually soft brown with understanding, quiet with patience. He leaned away, an instinct meant to protect, his eyes wide with the shock he was feeling. "What?"

Tom gathered himself, chained his temper, and spoke, "What kind of friend do you think I am? No...no don't say anything until I'm finished, cause you'll just piss me off even more." He raised his hand to make sure Dean listened. "I told you I would help you on this journey, quest, or whatever this is. I encouraged you to do this. I am NOT going anywhere without you. I will finish what we've started." His voice heavy with emotion, he continued, "I am....I am....I'm your Sam, Dean. I know how corny that sounds but it's true. You have something you need to accomplish, just like Frodo did, and I'm going to help you see it through. I can't do it for you, but I will be there when you need me." Tom looked directly into Dean's eyes and adamantly added, "I promise."

"So if you want to plod on, I'm with you. If you want to go back, I'm with you. Although I must admit the beetles and bats REALLY creeped me out. But that being said, it's your destiny, your decision."

Dean was speechless. Tears welled up in his ice blue eyes, turning them to a watery aqua. Never before had he ever felt so – he wasn't even sure of the word he was looking to express. What did he ever do to deserve this friendship?

Nothing. You don't deserve it.

Dean thought about the <u>Lord of the Rings</u> movie. He thought about Frodo and Sam. God, he hoped he wasn't going to have to get through the gates of Mordor or fight off Orks, but Tom was right. He did have something to accomplish. And maybe it wasn't saving the world or even Middle Earth but it was just as important to him. He was important. And he would have to do the work, but damn it, it sure felt good to have someone there to prop him up when he needed it. What would he have done without Tom to translate the symbols? He needed him. It was that simple.

You'll never...The imaginary hand squeezed the voice until it squawked and died.

Dean put an arm around Tom's shoulders and slapped his back in a warm gesture of friendship. "Man, I'm so glad you're here with me. I don't know what I would have done without you." And then he added, "Even if only for comic relief." He smiled, as he thought of Tom with the furry winged creature attached to his face. Then his blue eyes turned serious and he faced his best friend. "Really, Tom. I couldn't have done this without you."

Tom nodded, accepting the heart felt statement. Then he smiled and said, "So you wanna kiss now, or what?" And the moment was over, as the two boys laughed at each other, pushing and shoving until one fell off the rock with a thud.

Dean lay back in the dirt to catch his breath and tossed the words around in his head. He sat bolt upright.

"I've got it! I've got it!"

"What?! What do you mean?"

"It's not courage seek, wisdom speak! It's seek wisdom, speak *courage*!" Dean exclaimed adamantly. "I know it is!"

"Okay, so go speak courage."

"No, Tom. Think about it. In your culture what does everyone seek?"

"Wisdom. In this you are right," Tom replied in his most reverent tone.

"Right. So what does that leave?"

Tom started to answer and Dean cut him off. "That leaves speak *courage*. Doesn't it? Doesn't it?"

Tom started to answer once again and once again Dean cut him off. "But not just the word *courage* ,Tom, that would be too easy, wouldn't it? Wouldn't it?"

Catching on, Tom just waited.

"No, it has to be the word *courage* in Chinese," Dean finished, emphasizing the word Chinese by drawing it out.

Tom waited, not sure Dean was finally done.

"So? Tom? What's the Chinese word for courage?"

"Yong qi."

Upon the utterance of the word the ground shifted, sending the boys staggering to catch their balance. The grinding sound of rock upon rock echoed through the cavern and grew in volume until they had to place their hands over their ears.

"What the hell is that?!" Dean yelled.

Tom shook his head, keeping his ears covered.

Another shudder shook the ground. The grinding sound stopped, replaced with a sound much like that of a pebble skittering across concrete from the toe of one's shoe. The boys turned in unison toward the sound. Out from the ground, from within the circle of stones, a fountain of flames spewed, some reaching the ceiling of the cavern and then fanning themselves to crawl along the roof. The flames ceased, only to return seconds later, hotter and higher.

And then they heard a familiar sound. A deafening roar, ending with a high pitched scream. They had found Eternal Change once again.

They backed up to the wall of the cave as the magnificent cobalt beast rose from the ground, spitting fire and heat. Its powerful wings beat the air. It swung its regal head, glistening with scales of cobalt, back and forth, sending hot flames to lick the walls of the cave.

The boys shrank further back, moving towards the walls of the cave.

The dragon threw back its head, spewed a fiery roar, and then suddenly lowered its wings and came to rest.

Totally off topic, Dean said, "Well, now we know where the heat was coming from."

Tom just looked at his friend with a blank stare.

The Longgu Oracle hung around the dragon's neck. It was a large shard of tortoise shell with a hole at the top. A rope of silver threads around the dragon's neck held the Oracle in place.

"The Oracle is around the dragon's neck." Tom stated the obvious.

"Yea, I saw that," Dean agreed, still clinging to the wall of the cave. "Well, all I have to do now is go get it."

Tom looked sideways at Dean. He raised his eyebrows at the idea.

"Just got to figure out how. At least the dragon isn't throwing fire our way. Maybe I could sneak up on it."

Tom raised his eyebrows again and blew a breath out of his pursed lips, creating a strange sound.

"Wow, you're just full of ideas, Tom."

"Sorry, I'm just a bit........overwhelmed, I guess."

"Yea, I know the feeling," Dean agreed. "But I have to get the Oracle, and the only way to do that is to take it off the dragon's neck. Unless of course you have a better plan? No? That's what I thought. So I need to get to the center of the tar pit and then take the necklace."

"How are you going to take the Oracle?"

"One step at a time. Remember. That's what you said, and you were right. First, I have to get to the center. Any ideas?"

"See those stones? They look like stepping stones," Tom reasoned. "They look like they were meant to provide a path, of sorts."

Pretty scarce path. I'd have to jump from one to the next. What if I missed?"

"Mmmm, well I guess you'd sink in that black, oily pit of asphalt, and forty million years from now someone would fish your bones out and reconstruct you and put you on display for all the little future children to gawk at. They would point and say, "Mommy, did all late 21st century men have such small heads?"

Dean smacked his friend soundly on the shoulder.
"Very funny. I think you must be talking about yourself, pinhead."

"Oh no...not me...I've got a good sized cranium....lots of room for my super brain," Tom returned.

"Yea, whatever." Dean's smile faded. "Seriously, Tom. Do you think I can make it across?"

Tom wanted to throw out some quick reassurance but resisted the impulse. Humor was his way of dealing with fear. And he was afraid for Dean right now. But Dean didn't need humor, he needed an answer. "Yea, I think you can jump far enough, but if you lose your balance, there's nowhere to go. I don't know, Dean. It's your decision," he finished, feeling lame. "Just go slow and be careful."

Dean stood up and walked the rim of the pit, looking for the best path. Finally he stopped.

"What are you going to do?" Tom asked.

"I think this is the best place to start."

Chapter 8

Tom's heart stopped as he watched Dean's arms flail and his balance falter. Leaping from stone to stone had proved to be much easier near the edge. The stones appeared to be the same distance apart further in, but it was obviously an optical illusion. The last two jumps Dean made were running leaps that had Tom gasping air, holding breath, and then releasing, as Dean landed on stone. But this last leap had needed too much momentum and when Dean landed on the small stone his body kept right on going. His arms were circling like propellers on a plane, trying to back-peddle his body to the center of the stone. It was with a wash of horror that Tom witnessed Dean's failure. As if the world went into slow motion, Tom watched Dean plunged face first into the bubbling black. Paralyzed with shock and fear, Tom simply stood, while Dean slowly sank out of sight.

Liquid darkness oozed its way around Dean, tugging him, coaxing him into the pit. Thoughts of struggle were lost in the eerie sensation of being cradled gently in a bed of warm goo. Somewhere in the recesses of his rational mind Dean knew he should struggle. He should be fighting to free himself, fighting to keep his head above the smothering black tar. But his rational mind wasn't calling the shots. It hadn't been for quite some time now. Dean sank further into the sensation of oblivion. Thought escaped his mind. A peaceful calm settled over his body and mind.

Just let go. Don't fight it. Soon you will find peace. Why keep going? It's so much easier to give up.

Dean floated and his pain gave way to memories.

"Dean! Dean! Where are you? Don't move! I mean it, son. Stop right now and don't move!" his dad's panic stricken voice called urgently. The cave had suddenly gone black. Pitch black, void of any particle of light, black. A thin sliver of fear had snaked its way up Dean's eleven-year-old spine but was quickly relieved at the sound of his dad's urgent voice. Urgent or not, it was his dad's and that always reassured Dean.

"What happened, Dad?"

"My light went out. Don't move while I replace it. This is my fault. I should have stopped and picked up your head lamp and helmet," Paul chastised himself. "I should know better."

"It's okay, dad. I'm not afraid."

"That's good, son, but this is a lesson to both of us about what can happen when you enter a cave without the proper gear. When I get the batteries in we are heading out of here immediately."

"Dad," Dean drew out the word like a moan to let his father know his disappointment.

Paul shoved his hand into his pack and quickly felt around for a spare lamp, "Ah, there it is!"

Light filled the cave, chasing away the dark. Paul's eyes quickly found his son's. "God, are you really alright? That scared me! I've never had my lamp go out before. Good thing I brought my pack with the extra batteries. I hate to think about what would have happened if I hadn't." Paul knew they were far enough into the cave that backtracking would have proved to be incredibly risky without a light. While you're hiking into the cave you forget something as simple as how many boulders and potholes you had to maneuver around on your way. Going back blind could literally prove fatal. All it would take could be to trip on one rock and hit your head on another.

He took a deep breath. Never again would he be so careless with his son's safety.

"Come on son, we can come back tomorrow when we are better prepared."

Grudgingly, Dean agreed. He didn't see why they couldn't just use his dad's headlamp. It was working now. As if reading his mind his father added, "What is one of the first rules of caving?"

Dean thought about the class his family had attended. The Boy Scouts of British Columbia sponsored an expert from the National Speleological Society to present a workshop on caving for youth group leaders and parents. The youth were also invited to attend. Dean's dad had been very excited about it. The leader of Dean's Adventurer program, Tony, was a good friend of Paul's. They had met through their caving expeditions and struck up a fast friendship. Tony was one of the reasons Paul had encouraged his son to sign up for Adventurers. He trusted the man running the group so when the workshop was offered it was a given that Dean would be going with his mom and dad. So what were the rules?

"Never cave alone," Dean offered.

"Yes, that is one. Although, there are people who ignore that rule."

Paul waited.

"Always take the proper equipment and clothing. You never know what can happen in a cave!" Dean shouted with meaning. Looking pointedly at his father he added, "You messed up dad."

Paul laughed out loud. His son was such a joy to him. "That's right, I did mess up. So let's get out of here!"

Along the way Paul was very aware of all the possible problems he and his son could have run into as they picked their way around rocks, boulders and uneven ground. He took a large breath of clean air as they emerged from the mouth of the cave. Never again, he vowed.

Dean's mind was on something altogether different. On the path towards the cave's opening he had mentally gone over the list of equipment needed for every caver outlined by the expert running the workshop, Art Brehmer. He was very knowledgeable and obviously dedicated to making the caving experience a safe one. He was a short, stumpy man and he paced the aisle as he taught the workshop, often running his large hands through his hair as if impatient with himself. Hands that were calloused and scarred by the ropes, riggings and rocks he'd handled for many years. He had too much energy. He radiated it with every step and movement. His light brown hair was trimmed to a mere half inch, giving him the look of a military man. Who knows, maybe he was in the military at one time. He exuded confidence and a no nonsense personality that made you believe what he was telling you. But even with all those unforgettable traits, it was something else that had imprinted this man into Dean's memory for the past five years. His eyes. Bright green with dark flecks of gold. Large eyes that became extremely round and popped out of his head when he was trying to stress the importance of something. Intense eyes filled with the passion he felt for the sport he was talking about. At this point in the workshop Mr. Brehmer was going over the list of caving equipment needed to run a safe and smart operation. That's what he would say over and over again. Safe and smart. Make sure you are safe and smart.

Caving Equipment

A Discussion for Youth Group Leaders and Parents

Number one is the helmet. They can save a caver's life or at the very least a serious head injury. (his eyes really bugged out on this one).

Number two is the helmet-mounted light. It keeps the caver's hand free for balance and support. (more buggy eyes). *And of course works great for reading under the covers.*

Number three is hiking boots. Ones that have good support and non-slip lug soles. (only slightly buggy).

Number four is socks. Wool or synthetic only. Cotton encourages blisters and provides no warmth when wet. (not even slightly).

Number five is cave clothing. There were many types of clothing needed because there were many types of caves and conditions. The rule of thumb was to layer so if you got too hot you could remove a layer. You never wanted to be without enough clothing to keep you warm. (his eyes went from very buggy when talking about hypothermia to not so buggy when talking about loose enough to move but not baggy enough to catch on rocks).

Number six is gloves. Any durable glove, work, gardening or rubber will do the trick. (His eyes actually appeared to get smaller here!).

Number seven is knee and elbow pads. Just like skateboarding, you would like to keep the skin where it belongs. (Okay, this is where he got a bit weird, he closed his eyes all together).

Number eight, last but not least.... the pack. (The buggy eyes were back! with the added effect of a pointing finger!). The pack needs to have several things inside; spare lights (meaning an alternate light source, batteries (hey, dad came through on that one), spare bulbs, drinking water, large plastic bag to use as a raincoat when things get wet, pee bottle (eeewww, let's not go there), food, whistle, duct tape (for the fix it).

When Dean thought about it, it really was the man's strange habit of expressing everything through his eyes that made it so easy for Dean to remember the list. He could still see the excitement, hear the enthusiasm in his voice. It made Dean want to be an expert someday. By the time Dean reached the end of the list he was fully aware of how ill prepared he and his dad had been.

Dean wasn't able to breathe. But it didn't seem to matter. His lungs didn't scream for the precious air they needed. His throat didn't constrict in fear or a desperate attempt to suck air into the passageway. He was totally surrounded in warm liquid and it felt like he was floating. He spread out his arms, like you do when you are floating on top of the water in the summer sun, with your arms wide, feet stretched out. Something solid bumped his arm.   Then his leg.

Suddenly he was surrounded by solid objects that knocked into him everywhere. His peaceful calm disappeared when he felt something bump against his head. He reached up to touch it. His hand wrapped around a smooth object, round in nature, but not quite round. His fingers searched for clues, roaming over the item until they stopped suddenly. His thumb found two holes and his fingers splayed on either side, not believing what they'd discovered. Not able to help himself, Dean opened his eyes.

Tterror struck his heart, stopping it momentarily, and then setting to racing speed. Dean's mind didn't even wonder how he was able to see, being in a pit of tar, or how he was able to go without air, being a breathing human and all. What Dean's mind did wrap itself around was that he was holding a human skull! He released it as though the ghoulish thing had burnt him. It was then, in that one second of clarity, that Dean glanced around himself.

More terror clawed at his heart, slamming itself into his chest as though it were trying to escape the confines of his body. He was surrounded by bones! Big bones, little bones and sunken- eyed skulls with gruesome jaws that floated open and shut, as though they were trying to say something. The floating bodies crowded closer, seemingly arranging themselves into skeletons, dancing and taunting Dean.

You'll never make it. Give in .Let yourself go. What's the use? If these people couldn't do it then how can you?

A familiar voice in an all too familiar circumstance. The floating sense had disappeared, replaced with a dragging pressure that tugged Dean downward. He could feel himself sinking deeper and deeper. Bony, skeletal fingers clutched his ankles and insistently pulled him toward the bottom, if there even was a bottom. Dean knew he was being devoured, slowly, but completely. Once again Dean had to make a choice. Something he wasn't so good at. Until lately. And that is when Dean did something unexpected. Something the voices didn't foresee.

Dean began to fight back.

Chapter 9

Tom stood on the outer rim and watched Dean land flat on his face in the tar pit. And then sink quickly out of sight.

His shock momentarily stopped him from moving. He'd been watching Dean jump from one stone to the next, holding his breath with each leap, imagining Dean's failure to make the jump and subsequent plunge. So when Dean's over momentum sent him face first into the black pit it took Tom a couple of seconds to grasp the reality of it. His mind went numb.

But not for long.

The blast of flame licking its way over the sea of blackness rudely jarred him out of his daze. Enough to make him jump back nervously, catch his foot on a rock, and send him sprawling to the dirt floor of the cavern. He pushed himself up to his elbows, eyes on the dragon that had come to life. As if Dean's plunge into the black had somehow angered the giant beast, it roared and screamed. Its wings beat the air furiously and then it turned and looked Tom straight in the eye. Tom scrambled to his feet and took a step back.

The beast roared again and beat its wings, but no flames spewed from its mouth. No heat punched through the air. Again the beast looked directly into Tom's eyes; then to the spot where Dean had disappeared into the darkness.

Without another seconds' pause Tom propelled himself from one rock to the next, his eyes moving from the screaming beast to the spot where Dean sank out of sight. Still not sure if this was what the beast wanted, Tom kept a wary watch on it, secretly praying that he didn't become a piece of charcoal. The stones became further and further apart, but Tom was scarcely aware of the danger. All he could focus on was the empty black area of tar where he'd last seen his best friend. The best friend he'd ever had.

Most people believed that Tom was the better part of the friendship but they were wrong. Tom knew they were wrong. Tom saw what others missed in Dean. The inner good. The core of strength that had radiated from him even on the day Tom met him. A sad, young boy, moved once again, to another foster home. Completely unsure of his very foundation, Dean could have pushed the world away, retreated into a surly shell. But he didn't. When Tom motioned a game of basketball, Dean had smiled, granted it wasn't much of a smile, but a smile nonetheless, and accepted. That takes strength and courage. To accept an offer of something unknown when the boat you're standing on is rocking to hurricane winds. It would be much easier to plant your feet wide and stay put.

But not Dean.

Dean took a chance, moved himself over the pitching and rolling deck that represented his life and reached out for what was offered. Friendship. And in the two years Tom had known Dean their friendship had become unbreakable. And during those two years Tom had seen again and again the inner good in Dean. He never picked on kids younger than himself or smaller, unlike that fathead Denise the Menace. In fact, Dean went out of his way to help when he believed someone was being treated unfairly. Sometimes it got him into trouble. Well... actually, most of the time. Things would backfire and he would be left looking the guilty party. No one ever listened to Dean's story, they just assumed because he was a foster kid he had 'issues' and he couldn't be believed. Nothing could be farther from the truth. Dean *never* lied. He was impulsive sometimes, but he never lied. Mr. Desdale, the vice principal, always accused Dean of not telling the truth. It infuriated Tom. That pointy faced creep said really rude things to Dean regularly and Dean never retaliated, never. The good in him wouldn't allow it. He could have exacted revenge if he wanted to, he just chose not to. Maybe he didn't figure it was worth it or maybe he believed all the mean things Mr. Desdale said about him but Tom believed it was bigger than that. He believed it came down to the inner good. And Dean had plenty of that. And with that thought Tom landed on the rock next to where Dean had sank out of sight.

Another ear shattering scream pierced the air, punctuating the urgency of Tom's task.

Tom ignored the beating wings that created hot gusts of air that scorched his skin, making him sweat, and wipe his brow. His anxious brown eyes scanned the area, wishing he had x-ray vision so he could see through the thick black goo. How in the world was he going to find Dean? Fear clutched his throat, making it hard to swallow.

Another scream cut through the air.

Tom bent to his knees and thrust his arm into the blackness, blindly reaching for some part of his buddy to grab onto. His hand wildly groped through the sticky tar until it bumped into something solid. He grasped and pulled. The femur bone was stained and dripping gooey black strands. Tom screamed and pitched the bone back to its gooey grave.

What the......? Undaunted, he scrambled back into position and plunged his arm into oblivion again. Mao's words repeated themselves in Tom's mind. *The Darkness can swallow you whole. It takes not a part, but all that you are.*

Is this what great-grandfather meant? Was there no hope for Dean? Was all this for nothing? Was he going to be taking Dean home as a bag of bones? What was he going to say? To who? Was there anyone who really cared about what happened to his friend? What a sad state of affairs. To have no one in your life to care about whether you come home or not. Or to even care where you are or if you're safe. What was that like? Tom realized for the first time just how lonely Dean was in his life. How alone, truly alone, he must feel with no one to give a crap. No one to sit up and worry about him, no one to get mad at him for scaring them to pieces, no one to hug him when they find out he's okay after all, no one to care. The weight of it hit him like a ton of cement on his chest. And all of this just made Dean even more special. Even when he believed that no one cared enough to worry about him, Dean still remained good to the core.

Panic mounted, pressing the ton of cement further into his chest until he felt like no air could possibly pass. His hand blindly swept in circles until his fingers hooked a large object. He pulled. And fell to his knees with a low groan of horror.

"No, no, no, no." Pain twisted his face as he sat back on his haunches and stared in disbelief at the skull in his hands. Black oozed from the eye holes and as he stared, the jaw dropped open to spill more, like some grotesque horror show. It's not possible! It's not possible! Tom's mind screamed in silent agony, the pain of what he believed crushing his heart. It can't be! I don't believe it! I won't believe it! He has to be there. He has to be there!

Tom plunged his hand into the unknown once again, fear and frustration bubbling over until he screamed Dean's name.

"Dean! Dean! Deeeaaan!" The last time the word became a long, angry moan, as if Tom poured all the pain and despair he was feeling into Dean's name.

At that precise moment , Dean broke the surface.

Gasping and thrashing, Dean struggled with the black, gooey strings of tar seemingly attaching him to the pool of black. His blue eyes frantic and wild, he searched for something to hold on to before he slipped back into the Bone Yard, never to break the surface again. Dean knew that if he went under he would be lost in the darkness and there was no way he would find his way out again.

In his wild and determined struggle to find his way out of the Bone Yard, a memory found its way back into Dean's consciousness. One he'd put away years ago. That's what you do with ugly memories. Right? Put them away, keep them at bay, hoping they will just disappear someday.

This memory was of the same exhaustion, the same panic, smothering liquid taking all possibility of breath away. Feeling alone and scared. He made it that time, didn't he? He'd found the strength. And he was only little. If he could do it then, he could do it now.

But back then there were people who cared about you. People who would fight for you. Not now. No one cares now. Just let go. It's bett....

Dean let his anger wash over him. Angry energy is better than despair. Where did I hear that? But it's true. The anger surged strength into Dean's trembling arms, lending them the power to push through the darkness. His imaginary hand tossed the Whisperings into the sea of blackness. He allowed the flush of energy to wash over him. Suddenly the blackness seemed to have less weight, less ability to pull him down, less restriction to his franticly swinging arms. He could feel himself rising. He kept pushing with his arms and kicking with his feet. Like when he was a kid and loved to swim. Sometimes he would stay in the pool at the recreation center for hours, sometimes until the lifeguards had to tell him to go home. He loved the feel of the water rushing over his body, the sensation of floating with the water gently lapping up against his skin. There was nothing he didn't like about water. His parents were sure he was going to be a swim champ some day. They used to tell him that he was a fish and if he kept spending so much time at the pool he would grow gills. Then they'd laugh at their silly humor. Dean used to roll his eyes the way most kids do at parental humor.

The Whisperings washed upon Dean's shore once again.

But you gave up swimming. Remember, Dean? You gave up. You were such a disappointment to your parents. But what else could you do?

Don't listen. This time you don't have to give up. This time you can fight. This time, this time, well this time is different. He kicked his feet.

Dean suddenly broke the surface just as Tom cried out his name in a long keening moan filled with pain and despair. Wild, blue eyes locked on desperate, brown ones. Bracing himself with one arm, Tom swung the other in a wide arc, connecting with Dean's flailing left arm. His hand locked solidly on his wrist and he pulled back with everything he had, summoning strength from somewhere deep within. He also had the dubious task of remaining on the stone while pulling Dean to safety. The best he could do was to pull Dean to the stone and then jump to the next one.

"Come on Dean. Just pull yourself up onto the rock."

JUST pull yourself up? Please tell me he's kidding! At this point Dean wasn't sure he would be able to lift his arms let alone pull himself out. He dropped his forehead to the rough surface and took a deep breath. The cord of the pouch he wore slung over his shoulder dug into his skin, reminding him of the contents. He slowly pulled it over his head, each movement laborious and painful, and put the pouch on the stone in front of him. The orb was still inside along with the Living Bean and the Flaming Pearl.

At least something had gone right. If he had lost the pouch and its contents all this would be for nothing. Dean didn't think he could stand that. He would probably just let himself sink back into the black pit and into oblivion, never to be seen again. Facing a life of numbness, pieces of yourself scattered and disjointed, not knowing your own heart or *trusting* your own instincts, wasn't something Dean was prepared to do anymore. If he couldn't get this done then he may as well just end it all right here. Right now.

But he did have the pouch, and the contents inside.

And he would get himself out of the black tugging him insistently, urging him back into the Bone Yard.

In a minute; when he found the energy.

He shuddered, feeling the weight of an oppressive weariness pressing down on him. Why couldn't there have been a bridge or something? Why did everything have to be so hard, so...so...so impossible?

Dean's hand toyed with the drawstring of the pouch as he thought of a beautiful bridge. One that spanned the wide expanse from the edge of the tar pit, to the center where the dragon sat waiting. It was a wide bridge, wide enough for two, and it had railings and tall posts that majestically rose toward the ceiling of the cave. Posts topped with orbs that glowed to light the path. As he imagined this bridge, theLiving Bean spilled from the pouch and lay there, waiting. At least it *felt* like it was waiting. Dean picked it up between his forefinger and thumb and cocked his head. Behind him he could hear

Tom's voice but it was as if it were far, far away and being carried by the wind. A frown puckered the place between Dean's eyebrows and he narrowed his eyes. The bean fell into his palm, waiting. Dean stared at it, drawn by some strange force.

Suddenly he raised his hand and tossed the bean as far into the Bone Yard as he could.

The bean landed.

Nothing happened.

It sat there, suspended on the lake of goo. Gas escaped in bubbles with small *ploofs* reminding Dean of a witch's cauldron on Halloween. Too bad someone wasn't here to stir and cackle, and whisper throaty words to invoke magic. No magic here.

Just a bean sitting on a lake of goo.

Finally a gas bubble *ploofed* right under the bean, pushing it up to sit on top of a tiny mountain and then exploded, leaving a void into which Dean's precious bean was swallowed.

Dean gave an exhausted sigh and dropped his head back down to the stone he was still clinging to. Wrong choice. Now what? He half expected some unknown force to drag him back into the pit, into oblivion. The image of his bright and shiny bridge remained, but Dean could feel it slipping into his sense of hopelessness. He'd wasted the Living Bean. He'd used it in the wrong place....again. How was he ever....

Tom's voice broke through Dean's exhausted thoughts. "Dean, look! Look!" He was pointing toward the spot where the precious Living Bean had been swallowed up. Excitement made his voice higher than normal and his eyes were bright with wonder. "Dean! LOOK!"

Dean couldn't believe his eyes.

No magic?! Had I actually thought that?

Bean stalks rose from the darkness to form organic footings and pylons that spanned across the tar pit. The shoots from the foundations twisted and curled to form an arch connecting the pillars rising up from blackness. Thick stalks continued to send out hundreds of tendrils weaving through the air and plunging into the black tar. They pulled bones and more bones from the pit and Dean wondered with a grimace, *what on earth is going to happen?* The clacking of bone on bone filled the air, the tendrils moving constantly and quickly. It was like watching a living organic crane with hundreds of arms retrieving the bones and using them in its construction. Just when Dean thought this experience couldn't get any weirder one of the tendrils wound around him. Before he could react to the spike of alarm stabbing his heart, he was free of the black tar. Gentle sprouts and tendrils wove themselves around him, moving him through the air. Bones of all sizes flew past him on the end of at-work-tendrils. Some were large, some small. The clacking sound continued with slight pauses, during which high pitched screams split the air. The dragon had come to life. Dean's mind spun. Was it angry? Would it incinerate us to lumps of charcoal? Where is Tom? As if in answer, Tom floated by Dean, wrapped in his own cocoon of tendrils. He didn't look nearly as afraid as Dean felt. He actually looked pleased.

By the time the tendrils placed Dean and Tom on the shore of the Bone Yard the Living Bean had finished its job. The rapid clacking had ceased and the dragon spewed one last flame, ending in its high pitched scream. Stunned by the speed in which all this had taken place, Dean stood hesitantly, a blank look on his face. The tendrils released their hold and retreated as if someone was reeling them in. Dean felt barren and cold in their retreat, instantly missing the warm energy they'd wrapped him in.

He shook the feeling off; and raised his eyes; and took a step back. "Wow!"

Tom echoed with, "Wow!"

Before them stood a bridge that spanned over the black tar pit from the rim to the center where the stones stood, guarding the dragon. That in itself was amazing, but to add to the awe, this was the strangest mixture of natural beauty and darkly macabre the two boys had or would ever see. The foundation of the bridge was earthy and alive. Huge bean stalks and branches made up the supporting structure and appeared to, even now, grow and move. Tendrils constantly reached out, weaving and twisting, almost caressing the stalks. It was an organic base that was in constant state of movement; Life.

Intertwined with the living base, forming the deck, rails and newel posts. Death. Bones taken from the pit lined the deck of the bridge, each one interlocked with the next. The railing was also made of various sized bones, all interlocking, being caressed by whispers of tendrils curling their way in and around the bones. Life and Death. Can't have one without the other.

Dean's brain then registered what was serving as newel posts. Skulls. The skulls of whoever it was that hadn't made the right choice. Of those who lost themselves in the darkness and didn't find their way out. Dean shuddered. He knew how close he'd come to being one of those poor unfortunate souls. One of the ones who'd failed. And that's when he remembered Tom's voice screaming his name. Over and over until it sounded like it was tearing his throat raw. He remembered the feeling of Tom's hand locking onto his arm. The pressure of his hand as he pulled Dean to safety. The overwhelming sense of relief he'd felt when he broke the surface to the sound of his name being uttered in despair and finding Tom's serious brown eyes looking into his own. He turned to his friend, who was standing next to him staring out at the tar pit with awe.

"You really are my Sam."

Chapter 10

The boys' hesitant footsteps sounded hollow, like when you walk on a dock over water, or a boardwalk along a beach. The dragon hadn't moved since Dean broke the surface of the tar pit. It hadn't spewed fire either. Hadn't beat its wings. And the final sound that had erupted from its flaming mouth was the high pitched scream that had prompted Tom to thrust his arm into the sticky goo in search of Dean. Not sure if they should trust this unmoving, non-threatening cobalt beast, they stopped at the crest of the Bone Bridge.

"Okay, so now what?" Dean absently leaned into the railing of the bridge and crossed his arms, forgetting that his weight was being supported by the bones of the unfortunates that had failed the task of the Bone Pit. A delicate tendril snaked its way up the post and reached out to touch Dean's shoulder. Dean could feel its warmth the instant it made contact with his body and he flashed back to the feeling he'd experienced when the tendrils had picked him up and carried him over the tar pit to the safety of the rim. A sense of calm and warmth had spread itself deep into his bones. He'd never felt safer. Well, except, of course, long ago. When his mom tucked him in at night, after reading him the fifth bedtime story, she would say, "Only one more, Dean, and then lights out." And Dean would innocently nod agreement. But when the story was finished Dean would beg for only *one* more in his most vulnerable, sweet tone. And it would go on until finally she would look at him with *the look* that meant she really was going to read only one more. As she tucked him in, she would always sing his favorite rhyme, while she performed their nightly the ritual of folding over the top of the blankets so they just barely touched his chin, gently tucking the covers close to his body from his shoulders all the way down to his toes, all the while her sweet voice singing,

"A small tuck here,

A small tuck there,

Brush away a lock of hair.

Now my prince is ready to sleep;

I pray the Lord his soul to keep."

Now, as Dean's memory of the song came to mind it hit him, hard. I pray the Lord his soul to keep. Dean had been careless with the essence of who he was and now his soul was gone. I guess the Lord gave up on him. Or, if he was really truthful, he had given up on himself. Can't blame God for that. Sure would be nice if he could, but he was the one who made the choices that landed him where he was, not God.

A tendril softly nuzzled its way through Dean's golden hair as if consoling him or offering comfort in a physical way. As it wound in and around his curls the warmth continued to spread.

"Okay, that's just creepy, Dean," Tom stated with a grimace. "It's like they *know* you or something." His eyes narrowed and he stepped back. "And look at what you're leaning on."

Dean turned his head and came face to face with a skull. His warm, fuzzy feeling crashed and he quickly pushed away from his post. The tendril that had been winding its way through Dean's hair was left in mid -air, seemingly searching, then found its way back to the skull and slowly disappeared over the railing of femur bones.

Dean's gaze returned to the majestic beast sitting within the circle of ancient stones, atop the rocky knoll. This was different. This beast wasn't frozen in magic. This beast was alive. Unmoving, but alive. Its scaly body twitched with life. Periodically its heavy, blue lids would slowly blink over its deep, amber eyes and a small swirl of smoke would escape its large nostril. Climbing Eternal Change last time was like climbing a cold, solid statue with hard, diamond eyes. This climb would be much different. This beast was vibrantly alive, and most certainly more dangerous. It had the ability to incinerate him with a simple breath. He could become a tower of ashes in the blink of an eye. The Longgu Oracle hung from its neck, ancient in its wisdom, mysterious in its power, and very large. The tortoise shell it was made from must have been very old.

Yea, this would indeed be much tougher. Dean resented the shadow that touched the rim of his mind. *You can't possibly do this. You're going to fry. Turn back!* The Whisperings were harsh and urgent. *This one is **alive and hungry.*** Funny how the Whisperings always mirrored Dean's thoughts, no....his doubts. And not funny really, annoying. *Turn back, BEFORE IT'S TOO LATE!*

An ear piercing scream sliced through the Whisperings like a knife.

Dean's hands shot up to cover his ears as he threw Tom a look mixed with pain and surprise. Another scream split the air. Sizzling hot flames spewed forth as the giant beast extended its cobalt wings and launched itself into the air. Its paper-thin wings beat the air effortlessly, carrying the dragon in a circle around the outer edge of the cavern. Both boys stood in awe, slowly rotating in order to keep sight of the dragon's flight. Sitting within the circle of stones Spiritual Perfection was magnificent, but in flight its majesty was indescribable. Power and grace. As it made the circle its scaly body shimmered fluidly from cobalt blue to the deepest azure. It was as if the ocean, with all its color and wonder, swam beneath the surface of the dragon's skin, coated with a sheen of metallic sparkles. As it came around on its second loop, it swooped down toward the bridge.

Tom yelled, "It's coming for us! Run!" as he bolted off the Bone Bridge towards the first exit he could find. He wasn't real enthusiastic about the bat-beetle-worm's eye cave, but that was better than being incinerated!

Dean stood....transfixed.

It was as though his heart beat as one with each thrust of the dragon's wings. With every wing stroke Dean could feel his heart thump heavily against his chest. So hard it felt as if the dragon were inside him, pounding to get out. He was unable to move even the smallest of muscles. It wasn't fear that held him to the Bone Bridge like he had glue on his feet. It was awe. Raw, and utter awe. The dragon was magnificent. Truly magnificent. Power and heat radiated from the very air molecules surrounding the winged beast. He supposed that was the reason for Tom's insanely high pitched scream directing him to RUN! Dean knew he probably should be booking it in the opposite direction as fast as he could, but his feet just wouldn't move.

Eternal Change swept over him, its claws barely missing, and Dean remained, glued to the spot at the crest of the bridge. Fleetingly Dean thought, *missed me*, until something hooked him around the waist and yanked him off the ground and into the air.

Heat punched through the air like a battering ram, and Tom could feel sweat, rivers of sweat, running down his back. His hair drenched, he swiped the moisture running into his eyes away with his forearm.

And he ran. Ran as fast as he could towards the nearest exit. He could hear the rhythmic *whoosh* of the dragon's wings behind him, the sound of his footsteps as they went from the hollowness of the bridge to the soft padding of dry earth, his heart beating rapidly in his chest and the gasping of air his lungs demanded. What he couldn't hear, and it took him a second to notice, was the echo of footsteps behind him or the similar heavy breathing of his buddy, as he too fled destruction. Just as he reached the dark opening leading to safety Tom skidded to a dusty stop. He spun around. Dean was still standing on the Bone Bridge with the dragon swooping in toward him, its talons forward. Why wasn't he running? Why was he just standing there? Tom screamed out an urgent warning to run. He watched as the dragon swept over Dean, missing him. In the same second in which Tom felt insurmountable relief, he also felt a stab of actual physical pain. The dragon turned sharply, its tail whipping out and capturing Dean. With disbelief, Tom watched as the powerful beast started to make a half circle along the cavern wall with Dean coiled within its tail.

The sound of skittering rocks accompanied an uneasy feeling, like the ground was shifting, and Tom widened his stance. The ground shook violently and Tom looked down, wondering if it was going to open up and swallow him whole. He raised his arms out, like someone walking a tree trunk that has fallen across a creek, to steady his balance, and forced his gaze back to the cavern ceiling. Rocks were beginning to bounce down the walls of the cavern and dust drifted through the air. Tom sidestepped two small boulders that rolled toward him. Still, he managed to glance up just in time to see the dragon disappear into the emptiness within the ancient stone ring. With Dean somewhere in its grasp.

It happened that fast. In one millisecond Tom's emotions went from one extreme to another, ending in horror.

His best friend had been executed by Eternal Change. After all they had been through, all they'd accomplished. Gone. Just like that.

Tom dropped to his knees, and then dropped his hands to the ground, trying to support himself as the grief washed over him. Salty tears stung his eyes and rolled down his cheeks, some dropping to the ground, wetting the powder dry soil. Tom felt completely spent. His energy was sapped. The heat combined with the grief left him exhausted. He pounded the ground with his fist in frustration and anger. The ground shuddered just as Tom punched into the dusty earth, making him stop and look up. A familiar grinding sound caught Tom's further attention.

The stones were moving.

Tom pushed himself to his feet. Galvanized by some irrational idea that if he could stop the stones he could somehow get Dean back, or at least his body. Once the stones stopped it would be too late. Dean would be gone forever. Lost in the darkness for eternity.

Tom sprinted across the bridge, his footsteps hollow and empty. He ignored the grotesqueness of bone and skull. He ignored the soft tendrils reaching up over the rail. Ignored the very weirdness of it all. He raced up the rocky knoll hastily, cutting his hands on the jagged rocks. One frantic step at a time, pushing through the exhaustion threatening to remove his strength, Tom pushed his way to the crest of the hill. Just as he broke over the crest the ground shuddered violently. Tom lost his footing and tumbled down the rocky slope until he hit a large rock. A sharp pain stabbed his back just under his shoulder blade. He screamed out in pain. Tears wet his dirty face and his deep brown eyes glistened with moisture. The ground continued to shudder momentarily and then all that was left was a deafening silence. Tom knew the earth had closed and the ancient stones stood guard once more. He pulled himself up, wincing when his back stabbed him. There was blood on the stone. Time seemed to slow to a snail's pace. A drop of blood dripped off the stone and landed in the dust. It sat there, the ground unwilling to absorb it. Then, as if relenting, the blood drop disappeared into the dry soil, leaving only a spot of discolor. Tom shook himself free of the numbness threatening to overtake his body and mind. He had to look. Even if it was hopeless. He still had to see. He climbed, carefully picking his way over the rocks to the rim of the knoll. The ancients stood in a circle and inside the circle plates of slate formed a solid floor of stone. But it was what lay upon the stone that forced Tom to his knees and had him sobbing like a baby.

Chapter 11

It was the hottest summer on record, or at least that's what the headlines were saying. July had come in with a blast of heat that seemed to go on forever. It was the last week of August and there had been only the merest hint of reprieve from the insanely hot conditions. Temperatures soared until the pavement was soft and walking on it made your feet feel as if they were on fire.

"Well, Dean, one week til school starts."

"Thanks for the remind, Dad," Dean snorted. School was okay, but holidays were better.

"We're almost at the front of the line," Lori, Dean's mom, observed. "That didn't take as long as last year."

The Albany family was doing what they always did this time of year. Opening day at the fair at the PNE Vancouver. Free admission from 9am to 12pm.

"Maybe it's the heat. Keeps people home with their air conditioning." Paul offered, "Good for us. It's only 10:30 and we're almost through the gate."

"If I'm not melted by then. Man, it's hot. Can't imagine what it's going to be like this afternoon, Paul."

"We'll spend the afternoon looking at the exhibitions and then when it cools down at night we'll do the rides outside. Does that sound like a plan?"

Dean knew it made sense to play the day that way, but that meant he'd have to wait all day for the best part. So he grunted his agreement, silently resenting the heat and the common sense of his parents.

It took most of the day to make their way through the exhibitions, stopping for lunch under one of those outside cookout tents to enjoy their favorite Fair food.

Paul's mouth opened as wide as it could in order to take the first bite of his Smokie on a Bun. He had it loaded with sauerkraut, onions, mustard and ketchup and looked like a kid Christmas morning. "God I love these things." He took the bite, and groaned his pleasure. Lori was eating her usual chicken burger with lettuce and tomato.

"Mom, I saw one of those mini donut stands," Dean tempted his mother.

"I did too. Later....after I've had my good food." That was Lori's motto. Good food first, then treats. She'd raised Dean that way. But today, Fair day, was the exception. Today Dean could eat anything he wanted. He lifted his greasy double-patty-with-cheese-pickles and onions burger and took his first bite. Groaning much like his father, Dean's eyes closed as he savored the taste. With his mouth still full, he popped a large, greasy fry, dripping with ketchup, into the mix. He moaned again, deeply.

Lori cringed and then smiled. Her big man and her little man. So much alike, and yet different. It pleased her to see the bond between them. As it should be, boys and their fathers. It didn't always work out that way, so she felt blessed. "You both have ketchup dripping from your bottom lips," she said as she handed them white paper napkins. Simultaneously their tongues swept across their bottom lip and scooped the ketchup away. Lori burst out laughing. Dean and his dad looked curiously at each other, not understanding the humor.

"So, after we see the sand castle contest can we come back and go through the farm stuff where the pigs are?" Dean wanted to see the giant pigs. He was always amazed at how something so big could stay up on such little, short legs.

"Sure. The day is yours, son." Paul quipped, "There are only a couple of things I want to see for sure, the rest is up for negotiation."

The afternoon was spent being part of the thousands of people who jostled their way, like a human wave, down the wide thoroughfare, from exhibition to exhibition. Excitement hummed in the air. Children laughed, some whined with fatigue, heat or hunger, and some cried, finally tired of it all. Sticky- fingered toddlers clung to their moms, young couples walked hand in hand with gee-it's-great-to-be-here smiles plastered to their faces and families of all shapes, sizes and nationalities hustled hurriedly, trying to fit as much as they could into the few hours left in the day.

The sun was setting, the heat subsided, and Dean got excited. Time for the rides had come. Soon the lights would beckon riders. But before dusk turned to dark, there was one ride Dean and his dad had to try. Dean was finally tall enough. You Tube had lots of video clips and Dean had watched them over and over again. Each time the desire to try the Drop Zone increasing. There were pencil marks on his door jam, marking his growth, all winter and summer. The red mark at the top was where he needed to be to be able to ride the Drop Zone. He'd reached the red line two months ago. Thank God for growth spurts! Dean wanted to do it before it got too dark.
"Come on, dad! Drop Zone...remember?"

Paul's eyebrows rose above his glasses and he allowed his son to drag him towards Playland. They weaved through thrill seekers of every age with Lori trying to keep up. They stopped just under the sign that said,

Drop Zone $50/per person

"Dean! It's fifty bucks a person! You can't use tickets for this ride!"

"Dad," Dean's voice drew out the word as he turned to face his father. "You know it cost more than tickets."

"Last year it was thirty-five dollars, Dean. It's gone up fifteen bucks! That's thirty more dollars for the two of us. That's the cost of a pass for the whole place!"

Lori, watching the exchange between the two, decided to offer a suggestion. "What if Dean was willing to pay some of the cost? He has money saved."

"Yea ,Dad! I can pay for the tickets! I got birthday money, plus my paper route money."

Paul shook his head. "That money is supposed to be for special occasions."

"This *is* a special occasion ,Dad! I've been waiting for this all summer! I got tall enough in June!"

Paul looked at his son, trying to keep the smirk he felt coming, off his face. "June? Really?! Well, that's a long time to wait." He glanced up at Lori in time to see her expression before her hand came up to cover her mouth. Everything is so urgent for young people. "Well, if you've had to wait *that* long," giving emphasis to *that*, "I guess we better do this."

Dean wahoooed, and, jumping into the air, pumped his fist twice, totally missing the indulgent sarcasm in his dad's tone. "Let's go!"

Lori paced and worried after her son and husband got into the elevator that would take them one hundred feet into the air to be readied for their "experience of a lifetime." Once they were outfitted in their flight suits, Dean and Paul would be strapped into a metal tubed contraption that reminded her of a cat toy that was suspended from two steel archways by bungee-type cables. When the contraption was released, it would free fall one hundred feet....and bounce. And bounce, and bounce, all the while rocking and twisting. Who thought up these rides anyway? A crazy person no doubt! Lori was deathly afraid of heights. And that fear made it impossible for her to understand the hordes of adrenaline junkies milling around her. Why would anyone *want* to do that? The logic of it escaped her. Suddenly, a scream from above drew her attention. It was a scream of pure terror and mixed in with it joyous laughter. It took Lori a second to realize that the scream was her husband's, not her son's! She could recognize that laugh anywhere. Dean's laugh. The boyish, delighted giggle that so often erupted from Dean when he was his happiest. She burst out laughing herself. By the sound of her husband's scream, she wished she could see his face. Randomly, she hoped he'd removed his glasses. Oh, what she would give to be able to see what was going on up there! Smugly she wondered if Paul would still be as keen to get on Revelation – the fastest, most extreme ride in the world. She laughed out loud, again.

Dean's heart pumped with excitement as they rode up the elevator to the one hundred foot high platform. His dad was silent throughout the climb. The door to the elevator opened and they stepped out onto the platform. The scene before them was spectacular. The exhibition grounds spread out before them, which in itself was very cool, but beyond that spread the city, and ultimately the ocean. Ships dotted the harbor, the BC Ferries were docking and departing, with a steady stream of vehicles moving on and off the boats. The horizon was the most incredible shade of pink, graduating to blue, then to purple and the promise of night.

"Wow," Dean breathed out.

"It is beautiful," Paul agreed. But the awe was missing from his statement. Dean glanced sideways and caught a glimpse of something he never expected to see.

Fear. His dad was afraid.

"You okay, dad?"

"Yea, yea, son. I'm fine." His words didn't match his expression.

"Are you sure? You don't look okay."

Paul started to lie again and hesitated. Taking a breath he said, "Um, honestly son, I'm not feeling as comfortable with this as I thought I would. But...don't worry. I'm not going to back out. It's good to challenge your fears." Seeing the look of hesitation on his son's face he added, "Come on. Let's do this."

They suited up. The attendant took Paul's glasses for safe keeping and then strapped father and son into the seat within the metal tubing contraption. They were ready. The platform dropped away and Dean instantly felt weightless. Thought was not possible. Only sensation. A scream full of panic punched through the air, and knowing it was his father only made it funnier. Uncontrollable laughter spilled forth and Dean let the sensations roll over him. They hit the bottom of the cables and started their journey back up. And that particular sensation was the one Dean felt when the dragon snatched him off the Bone Bridge and soared into the air with him wrapped inside its tail.

The air left Dean's lungs in a harsh rush that sounded much like a grunt and for an instant Dean worried that he may never get air to enter them again. The dragon had a tight grip on his upper waist, all but stopping any air from passing into his now empty lungs. As if sensing Dean's physical struggle, the coil of dragon tail around him relaxed its hold.

Missed me? More like gotcha! In the millisecond it took for Dean to, firstly, realize he hadn't escaped the dragon's grasp and, secondly, decide he may be in serious trouble, a thousand things flashed in his mind. Important things like what is going to happen to Tom now? And then some not so important things like not having to hand in that essay on American poets. And then some really stupid things like how he was never going to have another peanut butter and mashed banana on a whole wheat tortilla snack. Who thinks of peanut butter and mashed banana just before they get swallowed up by a big black hole in the ground while they are wrapped in a dragon's tail?

Suddenly, the pressure holding Dean within the coil of dragon's tail disappeared. Dean gasped as he dropped through and landed on the back of the dragon. He grabbed the nearest spiky-thing for balance, hoping it wasn't as sharp as it looked, and planted his feet as wide as he could. It was from this vantage point that Dean could see the Longuu Oracle around the dragon's neck. Dean looked up. It was like a never ending hill of spiky stepping stones that led to the grand prize. Glancing down, which cost him a measure of confidence, Dean could see he had about ten seconds before he would disappear into the bowel of the cavern riding the back of this magnificent beast. Undoubtedly that was the direction of the dragon's flight path.

Nine….God hates a coward. Where have I heard that? Wonder if it's true? Dean hoped not, because he'd never thought of himself as particularly brave. But a coward?

Eight....time was running out. He reached for the next spiky-thing. And the next. They felt smooth but dry, and not nearly as sharp as they looked. And textured, like bumpy leather. Smooth but textured.

Seven....he reached for the next one but his foot shifted too far to the right and he slipped over the belly of the dragon. In that moment the dragon banked left and started its turn along the ceiling of the cavern throwing Dean back to the spiky-things.

Six....now Dean was at the apex of the dragon's powerful wings. He could feel the bone, cartilage and muscle working together under his feet. He stumbled forward, despite the movement under his runners.

Five.... he could see the strands of silk holding the Oracle around the dragon's neck. How was he going to get it off? Even if he got to it, how was he going to get it over the dragon's head? Panic and uncertainty shot through Dean.

You're never going to make it. It's impossible. Jump now while you can. You are going to die if you stay.

There was a part of Dean that wanted to listen to the Whisperings. Wanted to believe that he had done everything he could, so there would be no shame in jumping off and saving himself. The Whisperings fed on that part of Dean, pushing him to the edge, encouraging him to bail. But then there was the rest of Dean, lately becoming a much larger part of him, the part that knew if he jumped and ended his journey that he would never forgive himself. He would have failed. He would have given up and would have to live with that for the rest of his life. That part of Dean reached up and grabbed the next spiky-thing and pulled with all his might. "I'll worry about how to get the Oracle off its neck when I get there," he thought. "Until then.....just keep moving."

You will never....

Dean pushed the Whispering over the edge of his mind.

Four....Dean was only steps away from the Dragon's neck where the strand of silk lay...beckoning.

Three....Dean widened his stance once again as the dragon came out of the banked curve and started its dive towards the black hole within the ancient stone circle. Dean knew he'd run out of time.

Two....with no other option available Dean grabbed the last spiky-thing and launched himself towards the dragon's neck and the Longuu Oracle.

One....darkness descended.

Chapter 12

Thirty-one, thirty-two, thirty-three. Dean mentally counted the cars as they passed by the window. Red Mercury Saber, green Dodge Caravan with rusty fenders, beige slash tan colored Toyota Camry, metallic blue Mazda with a huge dent in the back bumper, and they just kept coming. Finally, feeling a wave of exhaustion, Dean gave up counting and cataloging the passing vehicles and opted for just staring out the window.

"Dean?" someone next to him was saying his name. Dean ignored them. "Dean," they repeated.

He still ignored them. Answering would equate to caring and Dean just didn't care.

"He won't answer. He does nothing but look out the window," the voice was saying, somewhat baffled, but patient nonetheless.

"Just let him be, "another voice offered.

Dean continued to stare. The next vehicle was black, and long, with curtains on the back windows. Another long, black vehicle with curtains on the back windows followed closely behind. Randomly Dean wondered about the curtains. Who cares about curtains on the windows? It just seemed so stupid. Dean was sure his mom and dad wouldn't care about silly curtains on the windows of the hearse that carried them to the cemetery. The car Dean was in pulled out to follow the two long black hearses. And behind, followed the hundreds of friends Dean's parents had made over the years.

Dean felt the bitter reality of being alone in the world, neither of his parents had any close extended family. His dad was adopted, with both parents gone and his mother was an only child who lost her father at a very young age and her mother almost ten years ago. Dean was raised not knowing any relatives and didn't really think about it a lot because his parents had so many friends. There were some remote aunts and uncles, but Dean had never met them and his parents rarely talked about them, other than using descriptive phrases like 'strange' and 'disconnected', when Dean had asked those few times. But now....it just would have been nice to have someone who was related, someone who might be able to understand his pain, someone who would demand that he come and live with them because they were, after all, related. Family, something Dean had always wondered about, but never worried about. Until now.

"Poor thing," the female voice in the car sympathized. "I wish I could do more for him."

"He'll be fine," the male voice answered. "Just give him time."

Dean doubted that. Doubted it with every fiber of his being. He'd never be *fine* again. But he never spoke. He just continued to stare out the window.

They passed a 7-11 and turned left onto Cremont Street. Several kids were standing outside the store, and when they noticed the procession they stopped talking and joking and watched. One kid, Leroy, from Dean's class pointed at Dean and said something to the kids. They all turned and looked. Dean continued to stare, right through them. Leroy waved hesitantly and had this look on his face. Dean would come to despise that look in the months to come. The look that seemed to say, 'he's damaged', the look of pity that preceded the inevitable, I'm sorry. When Dean didn't return the gesture the boy briefly looked down at the ground and then punched the kid next to him. The moment lost, Dean watched as the kids returned to their laughing and joking. About four blocks down the line of cars stopped briefly, then continued through the gates of Hillside Cemetery. The name was carved into a large stone slab with little angels hanging onto the letters H and C, as if they were going to fly away with them, leaving the words illside and emetary. Weirdly enough that thought made Dean smile. But only for the briefest of moments.

The car stopped alongside a row of graves. About four plots down Dean could see the freshly dug holes, side by side, with large mounds of earth next to them.

"We're here Dean," the woman's voice said softly.

Dean remained still, looking at the two mounds of dirt. Wishing he was anywhere but here. Wishing he could do a rewind.

"Honey, we're right here with you." Her hand took Dean's and squeezed.

Dean opened the door and got out of the car.

There were chairs arranged in a semi circle in front of the two gravesites and the minister stood in the center. Dean sat in the front, surrounded by all the people who loved and cared for his parents. He could vaguely hear someone sniffing. Another person was crying softly. Murmurs wafted through the air about how sad it was, tragic really, such good people. Dean continued to stare at the two mounds of earth.

The caskets were carried to the graveside by solemn looking men and placed on the stands that would lower them into the ground. The minister spoke words of comfort, tribute and prayers for the two souls that were now in God's hands.

Dean continued to stare at the two mounds of earth.

"Ashes to ashes, dust to dust," the minister was saying, as the caskets were slowly lowered into the open graves. Dean could hear more crying. People were blowing their noses, dabbing their eyes and casting sad eyes toward him. As the caskets got lower in the earth someone started to sob heavily. Uncontrolled grief erupted and the sobbing became louder.

Darkness descended, blotting out the vision of the two mounds of earth next to his parents' freshly dug graves. Sweet black oblivion claimed him.

In the darkness, Dean could hear the heavy sobs, heart wrenching sobs of grief being ripped from someone's soul. Vaguely, Dean wondered if he was hearing his own grief. The sounds he heard were a perfect reflection of the emotions churning around inside him. Emotions so big, he was afraid to let them loose. Afraid that if he did, release them, their intensity would destroy him. So he locked them away and put up a wall of numbness. And it worked. Until the mounds of earth. His grief flooded out, as if a dam had burst. His throat was sore and raw from his screams as they threw the dirt onto the graves.

Dean was waking up. But he could still hear the echoes of his grief. The memory of his emotional meltdown washed over him. He'd completely forgotten that day. Put it away. Erected the wall of numbness to protect himself again and kept it very successfully in place for years. In time, the numbness had transformed into something altogether different. He wasn't able to put a name to it, but whatever it was, it had kept him safe. So, he left it in place. But now, he could hear the sobbing, the intense grief, the uncontrollable anguish. A pure reflection of how he felt the day his parents were buried. He lay there for a second, absorbing the connection to the pain. Never had he felt a connection to anyone or anything around his grief. He had felt completely and utterly alone. Bereft and adrift a sea of anguish, with no way to shore. But somehow, he felt connected to the sobbing in his dream. Dean shook the darkness from the corners of his mind and pushed toward consciousness.

Still the sobbing continued.

Dean opened his eyes to the sight of his best friend, Tom, on his knees, with his head in his hands, sobbing loudly.

Chapter 13

Still brain fuzzy, Dean lay a moment, trying to understand the scene in front of him. Tom was still sobbing and slowly Dean realized that the sobs he heard just before he came to hadn't been the memory of his own uncontrollable sobs at his parents' burial, but the wrenching sobs of his best friend. Those were the sobs he had connected with. Those were the sobs that had given him something he'd ached for all these years.

Connection.

Understanding.

And a sense that he wasn't alone in his grief. This person, this sobbing person, understood his pain. A sense of joy soared through Dean and he felt utterly elated. For a split second. And then he noticed. Then he was horrified.

Tom's hands dropped from his face to rest, palms up, on his legs, revealing himself. Dean wasn't sure what he found the most disturbing. The dust covered, torn clothing that looked like it had been dragged behind a horse? The raw, bleeding cuts and scrapes that made otherwise young, healthy hands look battered and bruised? The small, dirt covered, tear smudged, oriental features of Tom's face? Or.... the hopeless, despairing expression haunting Tom's deep brown eyes?

Dean moved toward his friend on his hands and knees. Tears continued to stream down Tom's face in silence and Dean felt a desperate need to comfort his friend. "Tom, it's okay. *I'm* okay." He crawled closer.

Tom stared at him and then closed his eyes and tilted his head up to the cavern ceiling. Tears ran rivulets down the sides of his dirty face, tracing clean little pathways through the dirt, over his cheeks, slipping over the edge of his jaw and finally down his dusty neck. Dean edged closer, not sure what to do.

Tom's head dropped forward and he sighed heavily.

"Tom?" Dean tentatively asked.

"I thought you were dead," Tom said as he stared ahead, not really looking at anything in particular. He was struggling for control. "I thought you were gone forever," he continued. "I thought you'd gone into the ground with the dragon."

Dean stopped moving toward Tom, sat down with his legs crossed, and waited.

"I didn't know what I would find when I reached the top of the hill. I heard the stones close."

Dean could hear the fear and panic that Tom had felt in Tom's voice.

"When I got here and you were laying there, I just lost it."

"You thought I was dead?" Dean guessed.

"No, I knew you were alive," Tom corrected.

Dean was confused. "If you knew I was okay then why were you so upset?"

Tom looked at Dean and gave a quirky smile that didn't reach his eyes.

"I thought that you were gone, Dean. I thought the dragon had taken you with it into the darkness I climbed this hill just for one purpose."

"What was that?"

"To see for myself. So I could be sure."

Dean didn't know what to say.

"With each step, each breath, I believed you were dead. When I came over the edge and found you laying on the stones I lost it. But I lost it for a different reason, Dean. I lost it because after thinking you were dead, and that I would never see you again, seeing you was like a punch. A punch of pure relief. And then I just lost it."

Dean picked up a rock and moved it from one hand to another. He was overwhelmed with emotion. He had absolutely no idea what to say. So he did something that came natural. He made a joke.

"So....I guess you don't want me to tell anyone about what a sissy you are."

Dean could see the tension drain out of his friend. Tom held up his hands, palms facing Dean. "Do these look like the hands of a sissy, you ingrate?"

Back on comfortable ground, they both burst out laughing. Dean got up and held out his hand to Tom. "Come on. Let's take a look at those. Man, can't you walk and chew gum at the same time? How did you get so banged up?" Dean teased.

"Just clumsy, I guess."

"Leave you alone for a few minutes...." Dean left the remark hanging.

Tom smiled, shook his head and looked toward the ground.

And saw what Dean had clenched in his fist.

"You got it."

Dean followed Tom's gaze. He'd forgotten about the Oracle. Forgotten that he had grabbed the ribbon on the dragon's neck just as he jumped from its back. He flew though the air and landed hard. Hard enough that everything went black. Hard enough to break the barriers of his memory and open the gates. He raised his hand to look at the Oracle gripped within his fist.

"Yea, I got it." He let it fall and dangle. "So, remind me what this does?

Tom took the oracle. He looked at the script. It was cracked and rough, with several markings that ran the length in two rows.

"One of the names for the Longuu Oracle is dragon bones. Even though it is really made from the shell of a tortoise. I always wondered why that was. But now, looking at it, it does kind of look like an old dragon bone. The oracle is used for divination."

"Divi what?"

"Divination. The telling of the future, or more accurately, the prediction of the future."

"Oh."

"When it is used for that the fragment of shell is laid on fire and the resulting cracks are read by the ancients and recorded as predictions. But sometimes the shells were carved by the ancients to record historical events. At least, that's how I remember it."

"So....which one is this?"

"Well...it looks like both to me." Tom held it up close and squinted.

"How is that? Why do you think that?"

"Well, this shell has the heat fractures in it but it also has the ancient markings."

"Can you read them?"

"I don't know how to read the fire markings. Only the ancients can do that. But, yea...I can figure out the markings."

"Isn't it the heat fractures that I need to understand? Isn't that the future? What I need to do? The markings are the historical records, aren't they? How is that supposed to help me?"

"I don't know. All I can do is figure out what the script says. Maybe the key to your future is in your past."

Dean fell silent. Tom reached over and put the Longuu Oracle around Dean's neck. Then he moved behind Dean and checked the knot in the silk strand to make sure it was secure. Dean stood quietly as Tom inspected the knot, somewhat fascinated by its complexity.

"This is not your average knot," Tom murmured.

"I know. I don't understand how I got it off the dragon. All I did was grab the strand. I didn't have a chance to actually remove it from the dragon's neck. But here it is....fully intact...knot and all."

"Magic."

"Yea....magic."

"Let's go find a rock, eat some peanuts and check out your hands and knees."

Grateful for the chance to sit down and care for his raw and bleeding hands, Tom smiled and said, "Yea, let's."

Chapter 14

"Want some more? Got one more package left," Dean offered.

"Nope. We may need them later," Tom reasoned. "We can split my chocolate bar."

"Mmmmm....let's cut it in half and each eat only half of that. That will leave us the other half to go with the one pack of peanuts we have left."

"Sounds good." Tom proceeded to break the chocolate bar in half. He tucked the remaining half back in his pocket after folding the empty packaging over to keep the dirt and bugs out.

"Who would have thought, hey?" Dean mused aloud.

"Who would have thought what?" Tom returned. "Who would have thought two garberators like us would be able to survive on peanuts, granola and chocolate bars?"

Dean laughed. Tom was right. They both seemed to be bottomless pits. They were always hungry. Dean's foster dad, John, used to say it was because teenage boys are growing so fast they can't ever fill themselves up. But Janet, the nasty troll, wasn't so understanding. If Dean tried to eat between meals when John wasn't around she would screech, "Money don't grow on trees ya know! They only give me so much money a month for food, so you're just gonna have ta wait til dinner!" Then she would cook some horrible, indigestible meal that looked like it had been regurgitated by a bird. John would look at Dean and say, "Looks like Burger King's on the menu tonight." Janet would scream out, "You don't 'preciate my hard work!" as they walked toward the car. Guess John got tired of Burger King.

Bringing himself back to the original question Dean posed, he said, "No, but that's true. No, who would have thought that I would get this far? And who would have thought that I would have the Flaming Pearl in my pocket and the Longuu Oracle around my neck?"

"Oh, that 'who would have thought'," Tom joked, smiling lopsided and nodding his head.

The bubbling lake of blackness sat before them, spanned by the Bone Bridge, the island of stone in its center. An overwhelming sense of accomplishment washed over Dean. He remembered how hopeless and afraid he had felt when he entered this cave and realized the task before him. But now, here he was, after building a Bone Bridge, surviving the tar pit and riding a dragon. Yep...who would have thought.

"Are you sure your hands are okay?" To Dean they didn't look okay. Tom had several fairly deep cuts and his fingertips where scraped and very sore looking.

Tom looked at the palms of his hands. "Yea, they're fine. Sore, but okay."

"Maybe you should wash them with some of the mineral water." Dean pointed to the small stream running down the cavern wall a few feet away.

"Do you think I should? I don't want to get an infection. Or some strange bacteria."

"Well, if that's the case, we're both in trouble because we've been drinking it."

"Right."

"I think the rocks are more likely to have bacteria than the water."

With that reasoning presented, Tom went over and put his hands into the water, and felt instant relief. Because the water felt so cool and wonderful, Tom cupped his hands and filled them so he could splash his face, washing away the evidence of his emotions. He brushed the dust from his pants and shirt, ran his hands over his hair repeatedly to shake the dirt loose and then put his hands back into the trickling stream for one final rinse.

And froze.

That's not possible.

"Dean."

"Yea."

"Come here."

"What?"

"Come here. Come and look."

The tone of Tom's voice propelled Dean to his feet.

"Look," Tom whispered. "How is that even possible?"

Dean followed Tom's gaze and he smiled. "I'm beginning to believe anything is possible down here."

The two boys stared at Tom's hands. His perfectly healthy, smooth skinned, completely healed hands. No hint of the trauma they had just experienced existed.

Tom rolled up his pant leg and splashed water on his skinned knee and the boys watched the abrasion disappear, just like the special effects in a movie. Tom looked up to meet Dean's eyes. "Hmmph...." What else could he say?

"Yea," Dean agreed.

"So....." Tom started, "Let's get started on figuring out what that," he pointed to the Oracle around Dean's neck, "says."

Dean removed the oracle from around his neck and handed it to Tom.

"It really does look like an old dragon bone," Tom mused, "doesn't it?" He turned it over and over, several times, inspecting every little crack and crevice.

"Yea, it does."

"The heat fractures look like they form a pattern. Can you see it?"

Dean looked closer, but saw only an old tortoise shell with fine lines and deeper cracks tracing their way across the surface.

"Nope, just cracks to me."

"It doesn't make sense for the cracks to be there if no one can read them. There has to be something we're missing."

"What about the script? Can you read that?"

"Yes. That isn't a mystery. It's actually quite simple. The sentence, I mean."

"It is? Then what does it say?" Dean was full of anticipation. The Oracle was the one item Dean had dreaded retrieving. What did his future hold? Did he ever want to know? What if his future was something he didn't like or

want? What if....*That's right. Why would you want to take a chance?*
What possible good could come of it? The Oracle is trying to deceive
you....mislead you....

Dean was surprised to hear the Whisperings. It seemed
like, well, forever, since one had found its way into his mind.
His consciousness squirmed with discomfort. This thought had
no place here. These thoughts weren't welcome here.

Dean closed the mental door. Right in the Whispering's
face. And, side-stepping his doubts, returned his attention
back to Tom.

"Can you tell me what the script says?"

Tom was silent for a moment or two. He pursed his lips
and looked up at his friend. He drew a deep breath and let it
out in a huff.

"Your future lies in your past."

Dean's face contorted with a look of confusion. "That's
it? What does that mean?"

Tom just shrugged his shoulders and widened his eyes.

"Seriously. That's it? How is that supposed to be my
future?"

"I don't know, Dean. All I know is what it says."

Dean took the Oracle, somewhat frustrated, and ran his
fingers over the engraved symbols. "Your future lies in your
past......your future lies in your past...." he repeated, hoping
that if he said the words enough times their meaning would
magically come to him.

Nothing.

He continued rubbing the symbols and saying the words, more out of a need to connect the two, than any idea that he would actually figure out the riddle.

Suddenly Dean stopped.

He stared at the Oracle with wide eyes.

Tom followed his gaze.

And stepped forward in awe.

The tiny heat fractures on the back of the Oracle started to glow. It were as if the fire, from which it came, was inside the shell, and the flame was bursting through the cracks.

And the cracks appeared to have a pattern, just like Tom had suggested earlier.

And the pattern looked very much like a map.

A map of the UnderWorld of Darkness.

"Whoa..."

"Yea....."

"Amazing...."

"Yea...."

"Is this....?"

"Yea...."

"I take it I'm going to need this at some point," Dean stated matter-of- factly.

Finding his composure, Tom answered, "Yes. Nothing is for nothing down here."

Dean took a deep breath. The thought of getting lost in the UnderWorld of Darkness made him shiver. And that would be the only reason he might need a map. Nothing is for nothing. How true. So far, everything had served a purpose, right down to the food in their pockets. So, he would keep the Oracle safe, around his neck to be exact, and push ahead. He had managed to get this far. He could feel his determination outweigh his hesitation, and it felt good. Really good. Taking another look at the glowing cracks on the shell, Dean said, "Well, it looks like that..." he pointed to a small dark opening on the far side of the cave, "is the only way out."

Chapter 15

"You've got to be kidding."

Tom let out a sound of disgust.

"Seriously? We're gonna die."

Another sound, only louder, of disgust.

"Aren't you going to say anything? Are you just going to make strange noises?"

"What's to say? Like you said, we're dead."

The two boys had taken the only exit there was out of the Bone Yard. The tunnel was lower than most, but not so low that Tom couldn't handle it. They walked semi-bent for only a few minutes. Seeing the opening ahead had them breathing a sigh of relief.

But only momentarily.

As they left the tunnel and stepped into the six-foot-wide space the only way to look, was up. And that was when Dean said, "You've got to be kidding."

The boys were standing at the base of a chimney about eight feet in diameter. The walls of the cylinder were jagged, sharp rocks jutting out as if the chute had been hacked out of a solid chunk of stone with a jack hammer. Long jagged spears of rock stabbed outward from the walls from all different angles, starting about four feet from the base and continued for what appeared to be hundreds of feet.

"There's light."

"Yea, you're right. There is light," Tom agreed. Then wondered, "Where is it coming from?"

After what seemed like endless darkness, it was somewhat unbelievable that there could be light in this hundreds-of-feet-high tube. An inability to believe it would last settled over Dean. What if the light was lost half way to the top? Dean decided to keep the Silver Orb in his front pant pocket, just in case.

"Probably a phosphorescent substance in the rock. Like the sand in Tofino."

"Like the sand?"

"Yea, the sand in Tofino, on occasion, has algae that glows in the dark. When you walk on it at night your footprints glow. It's really cool," Dean explained. "I think this is the same kind of thing. Only the rock must have some kind of mineral that glows. Cool."

"I think it's creepy," Tom countered as he looked up. "The light is....eerie."

"Well, eerie or not, it sure is going to make the climb a lot easier for me. Can you imagine trying to hold the orb and make my way up that?" Dean gestured upwards, and then tucked the orb into his front pocket as planned. "So, how do we get started? You want to go first or bring up the rear?"

"Very funny," Tom snorted. "I think we can both climb at the same level."

Dean just smiled a dorky, insincere grin.

Tom hefted himself up onto the lowest rock spike, grabbed another one for balance and looked straight up. "Well, it's a good thing the water here has magical healing powers cause I think we're going to need it. These things are sharp."

"Great," Dean grimaced, "How sharp?"

"Not razor-sword sharp, but broken rock sharp. Come on...let's get this done."

This, Dean thought with disgust, is why you always have rock climbing gloves in your caving gear. Out loud, he simply grunted.

"Now who's making strange sounds?" Tom had already climbed several feet up the chimney when he yelled down his teasing remark, "And bringing up the rear!"

The two boys slowly made their way up the chimney one rock spike at a time, being very careful where they placed their feet. One slip could potentially have them careening downward, bouncing off the rough, sharp rock spikes. There was just enough room down the center that a falling body could end up being ripped open by the tip of one. Their hearts were beating like small ,captured birds and they consciously tried not to look down. Because of the phosphorescent mineral in the rock, the entire chute was lit up, making it easy to see how far down it was. About midway Tom stopped climbing and sat down, balancing himself by holding on to the spike above. "I'm beat! How much further do you think it is?"

Dean plunked himself down across from his buddy, balancing by also putting his hands on the same spike as Tom. "I thought you were never going to stop! Glad to hear you're as tired as I am!" Dean closed his eyes and waited for his heart to slow down. "I think we're about half way."

"Halfway to where?"

Dean didn't answer.

"Haven't you wondered what's at the top?"

"Nope."

"Why not?"

"Can't change what's there. No other option, so why go crazy worrying?"

One step at a time, Dean thought. *That's how you get through this.* Out loud he added, "You?"

"Man, are you kidding me? After what we've already seen and done, NOTHING would surprise me! I just hope it doesn't include creepy bugs! I hate bugs. Or bats....or fuzzy creatures that attach themselves to your face!"

Dean chuckled. "Is that all?"

"Well, no....small spaces. I can't do small spaces," Tom added.

Dean had to admit, other than the small space thing, he wasn't too gung ho to experience any of Tom's list of DO NOTS either. What struck him most profoundly though, was the level of Tom's discomfort. Dean had never, in the four years he'd been friends with Tom, ever seen him afraid. Tom was the rock, the steady one. Dean was the one with fears, insecurities and a sense of no control in his life. But things had changed. Dean felt stronger and was learning to trust himself. It was amazing, really. Amazing how that 'thing' inside you can shift from unsure to positive. And even more amazing is the feeling that shift gives you. A sense of power. Not the kind of power that involves someone else. No, this power is only about what is inside you. It's a power that sits deep within you and influences everything you do – every decision – every action. Yep...amazing.

"Dean? What's that sound?"

The fear in Tom's voice brought Dean out of his reverie.

And then he heard it.

It was subtle. But it was there.

Fluttering. The air moved, ever so slightly.

Tom's eyes widened. "More bats!" he shouted.

Dean reached out with one hand and clamped it on Tom's shoulder. "Calm down!" He exerted pressure to punctuate his words. He was very aware of what could happen if either one of them panicked. They were in a very precarious position. Bats or not, they needed to stay calm. "I don't think it's bats."

The air stirred, as if a small breeze had found its way into the tunnels. The fluttering sound gained volume and the boys looked up.

And sighed with awe; then, looked at each other with wonder. Then, holding on to the spear of stone, leaned back for a better look.

Butterflies. What looked like millions of butterflies. White, glowing butterflies fluttered in a coil, slowly descending the chute. Their delicate wings creating a magical breeze of cool air. Slowly they drifted down towards Tom and Dean and when they were close enough, Dean could see the intricate details on their wings. They were landing on the walls of the chute. Within minutes the entire cylinder was covered in magical, glowing white butterflies. Their wings were precisely designed in cobalt blue dots and fine black lines. Their furry, blue bodies shimmered radiantly and they had long black antennae.

"They're feeding on the rock," Dean whispered. "They must eat the minerals. That's what makes them glow."

"They're beautiful," Tom whispered simply.

One of the delicate butterflies danced through the air towards Dean. He sat very still. He wanted it to land on him. He was mesmerized by the magic they offered.

Tom's eyes rounded, but he said nothing.

Then another butterfly, and another, fluttered on the air around Dean. Soon a hundred butterflies were in the air, fluttering just close enough that Dean could feel the delicate, gentle breeze their tiny wings created. But still he sat – silent, motionless. One by one they landed. Dean was covered head to toe in butterflies. He closed his eyes and remained perfectly still.

Subtle, gentle waves of energy melted into Dean's body. It felt good. It felt magical. His body began to hum. Tiny vibrations coursed through every fiber of his being.

"Dean, you're glowing," Tom whispered.

Dean remained motionless for what seemed like an eternity, soaking up the magic that was coursing through his body. But curiosity finally forced his eyes open. And when he saw his outstretched arms glowing, his hands covered in butterflies, glowing, and the look of complete awe on his best friend's face he couldn't help it – he laughed. With such joy he thought his heart would burst with it. And when he did – the magical winged creatures suddenly fluttered away, leaving behind only a trace of regret for their host. Each butterfly found its way to the walls of the chute and settled to feed.

"That..." Tom started to say.

"Was, without a doubt, *the most* amazing thing I've EVER experienced," Dean finished.

"You think?" Tom looked at his buddy with a 'that's-the-world's-biggest-understatement' look.

"I wonder how long they stay down here?" Tom wondered aloud as he leaned back to look at them once again.

As if on cue, the butterflies fluttered en mass, forming the same coil as before and started to ascend the chute.

"Let's get going! We can follow them." Dean pulled his foot up to the rock spear he was sitting on and slowly pushed up while holding onto the one above. Tom followed suit, and with renewed energy the two boys continued their climb, until suddenly Dean threw out his arm and yelled, "Stop!"

But the warning came too late.

Tom reached up and grabbed the fractured rock spike, and then, with the broken-off piece in his hand, started his free fall towards the jagged spike waiting to spear him through his back.

It happened so fast Tom didn't have a chance to do anything but yell his surprise and fruitlessly reach out to stop his fall. He could tell by the expression on Dean's face that he was in serious trouble.

Time shifted into slow motion, allowing Tom the ability to register every detail, every movement. The urgency on Dean's shocked features created a momentary pause, letting Tom absorb the seriousness of his situation. Like in some crazy action movie, Tom watched, with disappointment, as Dean leaned forward, reached out, and missed his chance to grab him, as he plummeted towards certain death.

Dean, on the other hand, was not in the world of slow motion. Everything in his world was moving at the speed of light. He felt his best friend slip through the tips of his fingers, felt the emptiness as his hand searched for another way to stop Tom's future as a filleted fish. So he did the only thing he could. He grabbed the next best thing...a hand full of Tom's hair.

Tom's slow motion world came to a screeching halt as he suddenly felt like someone was trying to pull his entire head of hair out by the roots. He could swear his scalp was ripping away from his skull. The pain was so intense he wasn't able to breathe, consequently no sound escaped his lips and he believed his heart had stopped. Instead of falling straight down the chute, Tom was now swinging towards the opposite wall. He could see a stone spear ahead and had just enough survival instinct left to reach out to it with his feet.

Dean knew he was causing his friend excruciating pain. But the alternative just wasn't an option. If he hadn't grabbed Tom by his hair he would be impaled on one of the stone spears below, instead of gaining a foot-hold onto one of the stone spears only a few feet away. It was a good thing that Dean was able to use the momentum of Tom's fall to swing him over to the other side of the chute, which, in turn, minimized the pull on Tom's scalp. Dean was thankful that he hadn't ripped Tom's hair right off his skull!

"ARE YOU CRAZY!!!" Tom screamed in a pain crazed voice. "ARE YOU TRYING TO RIP MY HAIR OUT BY THE ROOTS?!"

Dean watched, with energy-sapping relief, as Tom found his balance. He smiled as Tom continued to blast him with his scathing rant. Well, he must be okay if he has the presence of mind to give me a sound verbal lashing. Dean wasn't offended. He wasn't hurt. He wasn't angry. He was simply relieved. So relieved that his legs felt weak. So he sat down. And continued to smile.

"What is so funny? PLEASE!!! Enlighten me!!!" Tom caustically spit out.

"You."

"Me? REALLY!" Tom returned. Now he was rubbing the top of his head. Pushing down on it, as if his scalp were loose and he was trying to push it back on and make it stick. Man his head hurt. Pain was still pounding behind his eye sockets, making it impossible for him to adjust his vision.

Dean lost the smile and his eyes turned deadly serious.

"You would have been skewered if I hadn't stopped your fall," Dean explained, knowing his buddy wasn't thinking straight yet. "I'm sorry I had to hurt you."

"HURT ME!" Tom repeated. "HURT ME....." and then he lowered his voice, realizing he was yelling. "That, my friend, is the universe's largest understatement EVER." Pushing his fingertips to his skull gingerly, he continued, "I don't think my head will ever be the same. Like, seriously, I feel like I just got an in-an-instant complete face lift."

Dean groaned....knowing he was going to laugh, and really not too sure how Tom was going to take it.

Tom's head popped up. Dean looked like he was going to explode. Tom took one look at his red faced, round eyed friend and totally lost it.

Chapter 16

Finally, fully recovered from their fit of hysterical laughter, the two boys continued their climb up the chute; being very mindful of possible flaws in the spikes.

Tom reached the top first; his scalp still burning intensely. The pain was motivation to not only continue, but continue carefully. He could hardly wait to get somewhere with a flat surface! He pulled himself over the edge of the funnel and collapsed on the smooth, stone-like surface. His hot skin almost sighed with pleasure as the coolness of the stone brought needed relief. It was a hard climb, and Tom was very hot and very sweaty.

Dean dropped down beside him. "Ahhh...that is so much better," he groaned as he stretched out on the smooth surface. Tom smiled. He couldn't agree more.

It was in that moment that Tom became aware of something. Actually he became aware of two things. The first being a large opening to the left of where they lay, much like most of the entrances they had passed through on their journey. Secondly, he became aware of a subtle sound. One that seemed to come from far away, but still held power when it reached his ears. A vaguely familiar sound. Tom searched his memory for where he had heard that sound before and when the answer came to him he stood and moved to the rim of the opening. He stood sideways to secure his footing and leaned out into the space ahead.

"Tom! Watch it! You could fall!"

At that exact moment Tom backed up, apparently startled by Dean's warning. His feet hit the edge of the opening and suddenly slipped over.

"TOM!!"Dean screamed, his mind seeing his best friend plummeting down an unseen embankment, or worse. He scrambled over to the spot where Tom disappeared and peeked over the edge.

And froze.

There Tom stood, his grin even wider than before.

Dean blinked. Then blinked again. He was having trouble believing his friend was alive and standing on a ledge only a few feet away but down on a lower shelf of stone. His alarm turned to relief. "Tom, I'm going to....." Dean never finished. The scene stretching out before him finally registered.

Dean's jaw went slack. Now Tom had an I-can-hardly-wait grin plastered on his face. Dean knew that grin. It was the revenge grin.

Tom's voice cut through the fog. "I thought I could hear water!"

Dean's heart beat heavily in his chest.

"How could this be? We just climbed Mount bloody Everest! How could this be?!"

Tom's grin got bigger. He looked back over his shoulder and then back to Dean. Now the smile was downright nasty. His face said it all. Dean swallowed, hard.

"Now it's your turn to sweat. Good luck!' Tom offered over his shoulder, as he dropped out of sight once again.

Dean stayed glued to the spot where he stood.

The beautiful panoramic scene in front of him did nothing but send spikes of fear racing up and down his spine and a very large knot in his stomach. His breath seemed to be stuck somewhere in his chest, unable to reach his lungs.

"Come on! The water is great! It's only about a twenty foot drop!" Tom taunted from below, ""

It wasn't the drop that Dean was worried about and Tom knew it. If anyone in the world knew Dean's biggest fear, it was Tom. Living on the coast had done nothing to change the way Dean felt about water.

He hated it.

He feared it.

He avoided it.

He wished it wasn't so, but there you have it.

Dean remained deathly afraid of water. So much so that he missed out on some really great chances to water ski at the lake last summer. Tom tried and got up, but no amount of encouragement from the other kids enabled Dean to move past his fear. Instead, he covered his panic with anger, and acted like a complete jerk. They were never invited again.

"Just close your eyes and imagine you are going to land in lemon Jello!" Tom offered in his most smug tone. Now Dean wished he'd been a bit more understanding! Dean had yet to find the humor in the situation. "I think this is a bit different!" he yelled down. "Besides, it worked, didn't it?"

Tom shrugged his shoulders and raised his hands in a helpless gesture.

"I can't swim," he lied.

"Yes you can! John told me so. You used to swim all the time, until something happened to scare you. Up until then you were like a fish John said. It was in your file." When did John tell him that?

"He said you were about ten when it happened. What happened anyway?" Tom questioned curiously.

"It's a long story!" Dean yelled, and even though he resisted, the unwelcome memories flooded into his mind.

~~~~~~

Dean couldn't breathe. A cruel, distorted face wavered above him. He blinked rapidly and the scene was lost in a watery blur. Suddenly he broke the surface and his lungs gasped for air. Then just as suddenly, he was plunged back under the water. Dean struggled to break the surface again but something was holding him down. Something pressed the top of his head further down, but Dean fought his captor. Fought wildly. He struck out with his hands, connecting with something solid. Suddenly the pressure hold ing him down disappeared. Dean kept swinging his arms as he broke the surface again. This time he wasn't going to go back under. He would fight this monster with every bit of strength he possessed. Just as he crashed through the surface of the water he felt hands on his arms and then around his chest. Someone was pulling him across the top of the water. Dean could hear his mother's voice calling his name. She was afraid. Her voice was full of worry and fear. And then he heard his tormentor respond.

And his heart stopped in disbelief.

"I got him! I got him Mrs. Albany! Good thing I was here to save him! I got him! Dean musta got a cramp or somthin' .I was afraid I was too late to save him. But I did....I got him!"

Dean froze. Did he hear that right? His mind called up memories of thirty minutes earlier, feeding his sense of disbelief.

~~~~~~

"Hey, maggot, what are you doin' here?" a well known voice sneered.

Dean, having just arrived with his mom, slowed his step and turned to look behind him. Maybe he would get lucky and his mom would be there.

Nope. No such luck.

"Hey! Maggot! I asked you a question!" the much older boy repeated.

Dean offered his explanation, hoping the boy would just leave him alone. "My mom and dad are looking at your new car." Unfortunately that meant the adults were all out in the front of the house, in the driveway.

"Mommy and Daddy. Your mommy and daddy,hey? You're pathetic. Get in the pool," the boy ordered.

Startled by the request, Dean asked, "Why?"

"Don't question my order! Just get in the pool! And start swimming."

Dean went to the opposite end of the pool and dove in. He started swimming laps and wondered, *what's up with him?*

After several laps he started to relax. Guess the boy just wanted to try to scare him. Well, it worked. He was scared alright. Dean was enjoying the chance to stay as far away from the bully as possible. Lost in the rhythm of his swim stroke and the coolness of the water, he didn't notice the danger at the end of the pool. Until it was too late. He could sense more than see, the body ahead of him. He cut his stroke short, but it was too late. A large, cruel hand picked him out of the water and pulled him up close to a face of stone.

"Let's see if you really are part fish like my dad says."

Without warning, Dean was plunged underwater. He struggled against his captor's strength but in vain. His lungs were red hot and screaming for air. Then just as suddenly, he was pulled to the surface. He gasped, trying to pull in the air his lungs so desperately craved.

"Nope, don't look much like a fish to me," the boy sneered. "Mind you, you do look a little green around the gills! Hahahaha!" His laugh was cruel and evil, and as he laughed, he plunged Dean under the water again. As he was going under he gasped for one last gulp of air but was submerged too fast and inhaled water instead. His throat closed off and he thrashed wildly to escape.

Blackness descended, and Dean went limp.

~ ~ ~ ~ ~ ~ ~ ~ ~ ~ ~ ~ ~ ~ ~ ~ ~ ~ ~

"Dean! Dean!" He could hear voices, like through a tunnel. Far away, but moving closer. His chest hurt and someone was making it hurt even more. He couldn't breathe. The pressure on his chest became more intense. The voices came into focus. Suddenly he coughed and water spewed from his mouth.

"Dean! Dean! Oh, God, he's breathing! Dean, It's mom!"

Dean opened his eyes.

I'm alive.

"Oh, Dean. It's a good thing Brett saw you drowning. He jumped in and saved you. It's a miracle he decided to come out to the pool," his mother rambled anxiously.

Dean couldn't believe what he was hearing. He stared at his mother in disbelief. She mistook the dumbfounded expression for shock and continued, "What happened, Dean? Did you get a cramp? I just can't believe how lucky we are that Brett saw you. He's an honest to goodness hero!"

Brett leaned down and put his mouth next to Dean's ear. "Say anything, and I'll finish what I started."

In that second Dean made a decision that would shape the rest of his life. In that second his life changed. He never told the true story. He made up a thousand reasons why he didn't tell. Firstly, he convinced himself that his parents would lose the friendship, then he let the doubts creep in. Would they believe him? Probably not. They would think he was confused about the rescue. They may even think he was jealous because of all the attention Brett got for rescuing him. Or ...maybe the boy was just goofing around and Dean was a poor sport. Anything but the truth.

He was petrified. He believed that Brett would find a way to hurt him. Dean made sure he was never at that house again. Shortly after, Dean quit the swim team, completely baffling his parents. Before the incident Dean was never afraid of anything. He had lots of friends and life was great. He felt good about himself. Shortly after, they moved. *And here I am, he thought. Good job, Dean.*

A voice from below pulled Dean out of his memory movie. "Hey, Dean! What are you going to do? Stand there

and think about how scared you are, or take the plunge?!"
Tom's question hung in the air.

Now, in retrospect, Dean realized his error. He should
have told his parents. He should have made them listen if, at
first, they didn't. He should have found a way. He was just a
small boy! His parents would have believed him. He should
have trusted their love for him. Now, thinking back on things,
he realized what his silence had cost him. He was robbed of his
confidence and that epiphany made him angry. That guy was
a bully and a coward. Dean spent years feeling worthless and
weak. If he had stood up and told the truth he would have
that to hold on to, at the very least. Well, there's no time like
the present.

I plan on telling you what happened when I was ten!"
Dean promised, as he shoved off from the cliff, slid down the
natural slide, and came rocketing out the end and into the
water.

Tom watched his buddy sail through the air in disbelief.
He thought it would take every trick in the book to get Dean in
the water. And even then, he doubted it would work. Tom was
very aware of Dean's fear of water. But what Tom didn't know
was, it really wasn't the water Dean was afraid of. It went
much deeper. Dean landed with a mighty splash that sent Tom
bobbing on the waves. Seconds later he popped up next to his
buddy with a mouth full of water. Tom knew what was next,
but wasn't quick enough to dodge the stream that spewed into
his face.

That was it. The water fight began. Tom splashed water
into Dean's face in such volume that Dean could hardly get his
breath. Then Dean dove down and grabbed Tom by the
ankles, pulled him off his feet and dragged him through the
water until he cried for mercy. Throughout the entire battle the

boys laughed and made their way across the underground lake to the opposite shore.

"Wow! Look at the size of those boulders! They are epic!!! It looks like a giant was playing building blocks or more accurately, building rocks!"

Jumping from boulder to boulder, the two boys made their way to a couple that looked like they were carved out especially for their backsides. "Perfect fit," Dean said as he plopped down on the one he decided was his. Tom settled on the one just above him and looked over the magnificent scene before him.

In unison they exclaimed, "Whoa......"

The sheer cliff ahead rose straight up from the shoreline and the tunnel entrance appeared as a black spot on the rock face. A natural , smooth stone slide started at the bottom of the black hole, dropped almost straight down for at least thirty feet and then leveled out to shoot straight ahead for another twenty or more feet just over the water, and ending right in the middle of the lake.

"The world's most amazing water slide!" Dean yelled. He punched the air and whooped, "And we've been on it! I swear that's the coolest water slide EVER!!"

A quick discussion comparing it to all the extreme water slides in the world kept them occupied until one of them noticed. Really noticed. And when he did, he jabbed his friend with his elbow, punctuating the jab with, "Look."

Tom followed Dean's eyes and sat in awe. This cavern was unlike the others they had encountered. This cave was bursting with rich, lush, green, foliage like that of a giant rain forest. Exotic flowers towered above the fan shaped leaves, reminding Dean of one of those movies about lost worlds and prehistoric creatures. Everything was over sized and mysterious. On either side of the tunnel entrance long vines hung in thick masses. Plants grew in little pockets of soil and along the rough edges of layered rock. Just when Dean thought this cavern couldn't get any more amazing, his eyes landed on the spectacular waterfall under the water slide. It started just below the tunnel entrance and from that point it layered down in three distinct tiers. Each tier spewed a fine mist that collected as droplets on the giant leaves. Glistening water particles floated on the air, creating a rainbow over the top of the waterfall.

"Holy crap," Tom said, almost reverently.

Awe struck and almost unable to speak, Dean added,"Yea."

"How is this even possible?" Tom marveled.

Dean wasn't sure he had all the answers, but he had some idea. Memories teased the edges of his mind, but this time, instead of pushing them away, Dean opened his heart and let them flood in. He closed his eyes and wrapped himself in the warmth of good memories.

"Before I tell you what I think, I'm going to tell you what happened when I was ten."

"You don't have to," Tom reassured him.

"Yes, I do," Dean stated. He knew it was time and he was safe. Tom would listen and understand, Dean was sure of it. A familiar voice, a whisper really, tried to find its way into Dean's mind. He completely ignored it and started his story. With nothing to feed it, the whispering disappeared. Tom never said a word until Dean finished by saying," I never told anyone."

Tom confirmed what Dean had taken years to understand, "He should have been charged! He could have killed you! You were just a kid! And to think he got treated like a hero! What a supreme jerk!!! I wonder where he is now? If we could find him...."

Dean stopped him there, "Revenge won't change anything. I'm just glad it's over."

"Yea, you're right. Why stoop to his level, hey?"

"Just being able to talk about it has helped. Thanks, Tom. Amazing how much lighter I feel, you know, not weight lighter, but...."

"I know exactly what you mean," Tom offered pensively. His mind conjured up a time when he needed to unload something very heavy. He remembered how good it felt once it was done. He also understood how much courage it took to do it, so he admired his friend's strength as well. He answered Tom's expression of gratitude with a nod, and then joked," Just call me Sam."

Dean laughed and punched Tom's arm, knocking him over. Before he could right himself he rolled off the boulder, landing on the rock below. Something caught his eye as he landed. Something at the base of the waterfall. There was a shape behind the curtain of water. A shape that looked very much like a dragon.

Chapter 17

He reached over and nudged Dean. "Look," he nodded toward the waterfall. Dean's glance followed Tom's lead, and then his heart missed a beat. It was there, right there, behind the waterfall. Waiting....

Dean searched his surroundings, hoping there would be another way, an easier way, but no option presented itself. A giant tropical leaf, just above Tom's shoulder, caught Dean's attention. A water droplet, about the size of a marble, traced its way down the center of the leaf, momentarily suspended by nature's force about half way to the tip, then it finally gained enough weight to finish its journey. Again, suspended by nature's force, the droplet clung to the tip of the leaf, as if waiting for something to happen. That's how Dean felt. Like a water droplet, waiting for some unseen force to control his destiny. He wanted more. And he realized, just now, that he could have more. He just needed to take charge! No one has complete control over everything that happens in their life, but that wasn't what Dean wanted anyway. He finally realized that is was what you do, how you act, the choices you make, that determines how your life turns out. Wow! Aren't water droplets amazing!? The world is reflected on their surface and when you look closer, all you see is yourself! Man, Tom would so laugh at me right now. And then again, maybe not. He was sure that Mao would be proud of him. His attention settled on the waterfall.

"You got everything? Some of this has been a rough ride."

For a split second panic gripped Dean and his hand flew to his belt. The pouch was there. He answered by holding it out for Tom to see.

"Looks like we're going for another swim."

"Looks like," Tom returned, determination hardening his tone. Blue eyes met brown, and an understanding was met. Dean stood, moved to the edge, and dove in.

"Hey! That's cheating!" Tom complained. Dean just smiled and strengthened his stroke. They met at the base of the waterfall.

"Wait until I get some practice time in! You won't stand a chance!" Dean predicted confidently.

Knowing he barely won the race, Tom agreed," I have no doubt about that!"

This new Dean was really growing on Tom. He felt that his great grandfather would approve of this new self assured Dean as well. Tom realized how much he resented Dean's fears but had acquired a new understanding about how it feels to experience fear...serious fear. He discovered a couple of his own along the journey and found out, first hand, how difficult it can be to control and master them.

Upon closer inspection the boys realized that the dragon was, indeed, in the waterfall. They also realized how much water was spilling over the ledge. "Tom! How am I going to get through this? You think there is any other way?'"

Tom just shook his head slowly. Talking was pointless. The roar of the water made it impossible to be heard. Tom motioned, like in charades, catching Dean before he hit the rocks if the waterfall knocked him off his feet.

Gee, thanks, Dean thought to himself. Then, with fear spiking up his spin, Dean plunged forward. Almost crawling, he pushed himself into the forceful curtain of water. It knocked him to the ground. He pushed himself back up. Again he was pushed into the stone ledge. This time the water picked him up and floated him over the edge and into the pond below. Tom managed to stop him there, saving him from being pushed into the rocks. On his fourth try Dean noticed something. He pointed to the base and motioned his intent to Tom.

"What if it leads nowhere?! Tom yelled as loud as he could. "What if you get in and can't get out!? The force of the water might make it impossible!"

That thought had already crossed Dean's mind and been tossed, but Tom didn't know that. Dean knew that there had to be somewhere for the water to go. Otherwise, the lake would keep growing and fill the cavern.

Suddenly, the dragon came to life. It broke through the curtain of water, revealing the pond behind it, and holding the Liquid Mirror of Mie Self in its claws, as if offering it to Dean

Dean hesitated.

Eternal Change threw back its shimmering cobalt head and spewed hot flames. Water sizzled, steamed and boiled. The humidity in the cavern shot up tenfold. And then Eternal Change spoke. The now familiar roar, ending in a high pitched scream, once again startled the boys.

They both froze.

The dragon moved back, once again breaking through the heavy curtain of water, revealing the cave behind.

Afraid he'd lost his chance to get the mirror, Dean bolted towards the base, ready to dive in. Tom grabbed his shirt and pulled, hard. Dean came off his feet and landed on his butt in the water. Shocked and somewhat desperate he yelled, "What are you doing? I'm going to miss my chance!"

"Dean! I need to tell you something!" Tom yelled back.

"NOW?! You need to tell me NOW!? Dean yelled in exasperation.

"YES! NOW!"

"Okay! But hurry!"

Eternal Change spoke again, as if to punctuate Dean's words. His eyebrow rose with marked meaning.

"I need to tell you about the Legend of the Chamber of Souls! Tom continued.

Dean just stood and waited.

"When you get the Liquid Mirror of Mie Self you need to go to the Chamber of Souls and catch your reflection in it."

Dean's tone was impatient," I know all that! You already told me!"

"But there is something I didn't tell you," Tom interrupted.

Dean looked at his friend and squinted "You mean didn't tell me like you didn't tell me that Spiritual Perfection was a dragon, didn't tell me?"

Tom looked down at the water.

Dean's stomach dropped into his feet. *Now What?!!*

"The Chamber of Souls is guarded by the Soul Master."

Dean nodded.

"The Soul Master will ask you for the three objects before he will give entry to the Chamber."

Dean nodded.

"The Soul Master is a combination of two things."

Dean nodded.

Tom took a deep breath and finished.

"He sits on the Throne at the entrance."

Dean nodded impatiently, directing a warning look toward Tom.

"He has a giant bat-like head and the body of a cricket, a giant cricket," Tom finished.

Well, you have to have a giant body if you have a giant head, don't you! Dean practically sneered to himself.

Aloud Dean shouted, "AND I HAVE TO GET PAST HIM!"

Tom didn't know what to say.

"AND I HAVE TO GET PAST HIM!" Dean repeated.

Tom just nodded.

"Don't crickets have wings? And really weird legs? And bats...well we both know all about bats! DON'T WE?!! You wait until now to tell me this!?"

Tom nodded again.

As frustrated as Dean was, he knew exactly why Tom hadn't told him. The same reason he didn't tell him about the dragons earlier. He was afraid he wouldn't follow through.

And, he was probably right. Had he known then what he knew now there was no way he would have left Mao's chamber and stepped into the tunnels.

"Okay, I get why. Any suggestions or things I should know now?"

"All I know is what he looks like, that you will need the three objects. The Liquid Mirror is the last one. You already have the Flaming Pearl and Longuu Oracle. Once you are in the Chamber of Souls you are on your own. I don't think I can go there with you."

Eternal Change snorted, releasing a long, curly trail of smoke.

Dean knew time was running out so he took a deep breath, before he could change his mind, and dove into the opening. Dean's body cut through the water like a knife, making him wonder if maybe this was going to be easier than he thought. For about thirty seconds. Then he felt the pull of a very strong current. Strong enough to pull him under the surface, spin him several times and then force him to the bottom. Dean struggled against the force of water as vivid memories assaulted his mind. The hand holding him under this time was the force of nature, but just as powerful, if not more so. Dean remembered how hard he tried to hold his breath, and repeated the strategy. Unfortunately Dean couldn't swing his arms and punch the waterfall until it let go. He was going to have to overcome the powerful pressure holding him down. And he was going to have to hold his breath while he did it. He popped to the surface, being careful not to get a mouthful of water. He took a deep breath. Once again the turbulent water pulled him under. With his lungs full of air, Dean took the opportunity to open his eyes and search for the opening. Then he went up for more air. His body was being rolled and swirled in a small whirl pool. It was hard for him to focus on any one spot. He could feel the pull of another strong current and prepared himself. This time Dean knew what to do. Instead of fighting the current he decided to ride the current. He became one with the force of the water. On his third lap Dean found the opening and, with his eyes on the prize, he started counting, 1….2….3….4….5. On five he rode the current one more time and when he reached the magic number he broke away from the eddy and dove under the water, and ran right smack into a boulder.

OUCH! I'm never going to be able to do this!

Yes, you will. You've done so much. Don't give up. Dean could hear his dad's voice in his head, encouraging him to the top of the hill they had decided to explore while visiting a cavern in a national park. Dean ran out of energy near the top and complained that he couldn't do the rest. He wanted to start back down. His father encouraged and helped his son and ultimately they both finished the climb. That was the voice Dean could hear. The other Whispering didn't exist anymore. He focused on his father's words and got ready for another spin in the whirlpool. 1...2...3...4...5! He threw himself at the opening. Eternal Change screamed and beat its wings, interrupting the water flow just enough to give Dean a chance to dive into the opening.

He popped up several yards away, inside the cave, gasping for air. He coughed violently, until the inhaled water was expelled. Needing to find solid ground, Dean swam towards the dragon. From this position he could only see the back of Eternal Change, which included its long, thick tail, with spiky things running from the tip to the top of his cobalt head. And it was moving. It was swishing back and forth in the water, in a self soothing manner. Dean reached the shallows and stood, ready to run if Eternal Change became more aggressive. Dean flattened himself to the wall of the cavern and slowly moved toward the front of the dragon. The cavern wall was smooth and cool to the touch. This cavern was much smaller than the others. More like a cave, really. But this cavern was awe inspiring. This cavern was made entirely of white coral, the most beautiful formation created in the underground world. The walls reflected the azure blue of the water Dean was floating in, and somehow glittered as if there was a source of light above. Then Dean remembered. Florescent algae. That's got to be it. The minerals in the coral and water create an inner light source. It was spectacular!! The dragon's tail moved, nudging Dean out of his mesmerized state. He continued to inch his way toward the front of the dragon

Suddenly the dragon's tail rose up and slapped down on the water, creating a wave that washed Dean off the ledge. *NOW WHAT!* Dean thought , in frustration. The dragon snorted, threw back its head and spewed waves of fire. Dean said, Okay, okay, I get the message." He pulled himself out of the water onto the ledge and, with purpose, strode towards the front of the cave.

"Okay, buddy! Hand it over!" Dean yelled, as he reached the front of the dragon. Eternal Change swung its head around, its sapphire eyes sparkling brightly, and looked directly at Dean. Deep within there was a challenge Dean accepted. Ignoring the lesser volume of water pouring over the entrance, Dean stepped toward Eternal Change.

And found nothing. The mirror wasn't there. Nothing rested within the claws of the dragon. What?! Where did it go? I'm too late. Dean felt a sickness in the pit of his stomach.
Then he remembered what Mao said earlier. *It's never too late,* and the sickness abated. But the mirror isn't here?!

Once again Mao's voice echoed in his mind. *Your path may not always be obvious, but it is always before you.*

Dean didn't get it. What does that have to do with this? Totally frustrated, Dean growled. Eternal Change looked him in the eye and Dean felt like he was swimming in a sea of sapphire.

Then he remembered something else. A door where there was no door. A trapdoor where there was no trapdoor. As if, just believing it was there was enough to create its existence!

Dean stepped in front of Eternal Change and reached out to take the Liquid Mirror of Mie Self. The frame materialized under Dean's trembling grip. A mirror where there was no mirror. Go figure. Eternal Change snorted, releasing another swirl of smoke.

And for Dean, the world went black.

Chapter 18

Tom watched Dean dive into the water and marveled at how far his friend had come. For a guy who avoided water at all cost he sure seemed comfortable in it now! He watched Dean struggle with the current until he decided to use it to his advantage.

Smart.

He watched as his friend noticed something, apparently an opening, under the rock ledge.

Observant.

He watched as Dean figured out the timing needed to break free of the whirlpool he was trapped in.

And he watched as Dean ran smack into the rock.

Wrong.

He watched as Dean adjusted his strategy and tried again.

Tenacious.

He rejoiced as Dean disappeared under the rock ledge, and then he started to worry. What if he runs out of air? What if the dragon roasts him to a crispy critter? Just....What if?! Then he saw Dean....inching his way towards the front of the dragon. That's when Tom noticed. The mirror wasn't there! What happened to the mirror?! Tom yelled out to Dean, but he knew he couldn't hear over the roar of the waterfall. He was wasting his breath. They were too late. The Liquid Mirror of Mie Self was gone. Tom sat down in despair. After all they had been through! It just wasn't fair! He slapped the rock beside him. His hand stung from the impact. Dean deserved the mirror. He'd worked hard, done everything asked of him! He ran his hands through his hair and grabbed two handfuls and pulled. And that was when he noticed Dean in front of Eternal Change. He missed how he got there! What was he doing? The mirror wasn't.....Tom couldn't finish the thought. When Dean reached into the waterfall, for a mirror that wasn't there, it materialized within his grasp.

Then Dean disappeared. Mirror and all.

Chapter 19

Dean opened his eyes; and dropped the mirror.

Before him was a creature of the exact description Tom gave just a few minutes earlier. Only bigger. Much bigger. It was sitting on a throne made of the most amazing combination of flowstones and cavern coral he had ever seen, even if you counted all the books he had on the subject. He was stunned, not only by the beauty of it, but the size. He stepped back to get a better overall look, not to mention putting some distance between himself and what he guessed was, the Soul Master, Dean's heart pounded so hard he was sure it could be heard by those pointed bat ears. Expecting the creature to move any minute, Dean readied himself to run. He surveyed the cavern and found nothing. No entrance....no exit. *Now what?* Dean thought. Unlike the dragons; they always seemed to sense when Dean needed a nudge, or clue, the giant cricket with a bat-like head just sat there. Dean squinted and took a closer look. And couldn't believe his eyes...or his luck.

It was a statue. A statue made of stone, intricately carved, and postured in such a way that no one would ever suspect it wasn't real. It sat upon a Throne with its bat-like left wing resting on the arm. The skin between the two ribs on the wing formed a perfect pocket. The carved inset design on his chest was a perfect replica of the Longuu Oracle. Everything came together. Everything made sense. He reached into the velvet pouch on his belt and pulled out the Flaming Pearl. He placed it in the pocket. Instantly, blue flame engulfed the pearl. It danced, as if joyful to be set free once again. Blue flames licked their way up the pearl and when reaching the top, separated from the pearl to dance in individual flames to the ceiling of the cave. The cavern walls glowed and glittered with radiant blue sparkles. When Dean removed the Longuu oracle from the pouch the magic knot released. Dean reached up to place the liver braid around the statue's neck. This close,

Dean admired the craftsmanship in the details of the statue. Every line, wrinkle and the eyes....blinked! Dean was so startled he lost his balance and fell off the throne, landing next to the mirror. Scrambling backward, like a crab, he kept his eyes on the enormous creature in front of him. It blinked again.

Beams of light and fire shot out from around the Oracle, as if it were going to explode. Then, the Soul Master stood; and looked right at Dean. The earth began to shake. Dean adjusted his stance, intent on staying on his feet. The earth's movement, and sound of rock scraping rock, had a familiar feel.

The Bone Yard. Is there another dragon?

The ground shook again. The Throne shifted and began to rise. Dean watched in awe, as the thing he had been searching for all this time, was revealed.

The entrance to the Chamber of Souls. He was sure of it.

The Soul Master spread its cricket-like wings, uttered a high pitched scream, and repositioned itself on the Throne.

I guess that's my cue, Dean thought. He headed toward the opening under the Throne, scooping up the mirror on his way, and entered the Chamber of Souls.

Chapter 20

The Chamber of Souls was not what Dean expected. He wasn't sure what he expected, but it wasn't this. Once he entered the chamber the world went black....for the second time.

Something brushed against his arm and he spun around, searching the darkness. Something was there, Dean could sense it. Or someone. He didn't want to think about what might be lurking in the shadows. The Chamber of Souls was already frightening enough. Something touched his shoulder and he spun again. Now his ear, and he swiped at it as if it were a bug. *Am I alone in here? It sure doesn't feel like it.* He strode to the wall closest to him in an attempt to get away from who or whatever it was touching him. He tried several locations but each time the touch would find him.

And then the first emotion hit him. Like a freight train.

Sadness. Overwhelming sadness. He recognized it because it had been his constant companion for the last two years. Dean moved away from the wall, desperately wanting to avoid the emotion assaulting him. As if it were something physical that he could escape.

Memories flooded his mind. Memories of when he was just a small child, and everything was right in his life. Time spent with his mom and dad on camping trips, exploring caverns and visiting theme parks along the way. Evening meals, during which, his parents would discuss the day and laugh and sometimes scold and even sometimes fight. Dean pushed the painful memories away, just like he'd been doing for the last two years. Powerful memories like the one of his mom tucking him every night while she sang the verse she made up when he was only a year old. The familiar stab of pain came, just like Dean expected. He tried to dodge it by moving further down the cave wall. But it followed him. He smacked the wall with his open hand. The sting brought tears to his eyes. Then something washed over him. Anger.

He was so angry that he screamed out, "GO AWAY! LEAVE ME ALONE!" More memories washed over him, feeding his anger. Memories of the night his parents died. The night he was supposed to go to the movies with them and didn't. He was with his friends. His stomach lurched and he felt like he was going to get sick.

"I SAID GO AWAY!!" He tried to push the agonizing memories back to where he'd stored them for the past two years. Coming home from the mall to find a police car parked in front of his home, the looks on the faces of the cops that got out of the car and started toward him. They looked at the mother who had given him a ride home and then at each other. The expression told a story of regret and longing. Like they would rather be anywhere but here, in this moment. The words they spoke meant nothing to him because Dean couldn't hear them. His mind had shut down. The words, *your parents have been in an accident,* didn't compute. His brain had stalled. Anger swelled and made it painful for Dean to breath.

He hit the wall of the cave again and screamed, "WHY ME? What did I do to deserve this?! I just wanted to be with my friends! There's nothing wrong with that!"

But Dean didn't believe what he was saying. He believed that if he had gone to the movies with his parents they probably wouldn't have been in a car crash. Regret stabbed his heart. It would have been his last time to see his parents; and it would have been a good time. But Dean thought it would be boring, so he opted to go with his friends to some game center. If he had gone with them they probably would have stopped somewhere for ice cream. Movie nights were the best times. Dean was allowed popcorn and pop at the movies and ice cream on the way home. But he wasn't with them, so they didn't stop for ice cream. If they had, they wouldn't have been in the intersection when the drunk ran the red light. It was his fault. Guilt washed over Dean in waves until his knees buckled and he slid down the wall until he was able to wrap his arms around his knees. He propped the Liquid Mirror of Mie Self against the opposite cavern wall. And fell apart.

~ ~

When the police told Dean about his parents, he never cried. When the social worker came to pick him up, he never cried. When strangers took him to his parents' funeral, he never cried. When he was taken to his first foster home, he never cried, nor did he cry at any of the various others. When John left his wife, the troll, leaving Dean by himself, he never cried. People commented on what a strong boy he was. It was like they were relieved that they didn't have to deal with his grief. He was repeatedly told," It will be alright." And that was a lie. It would never be alright again and Dean knew it. He ached for his parents and despite everyone's efforts he wasn't responding. He pulled further and further inside himself, until there was nothing left to save. He wasn't able to get past the overwhelming fear that had taken him over. Having given in to fear once before, it was easy to do it again. He was afraid that if he ever allowed himself to cry again, like he did at his parents' graveside, he would never be able to stop. And who would be there to comfort him? Who would soothe his pain? And he would be vulnerable, very vulnerable, and he wasn't willing to take that chance. He had allowed fear to dominate his life ever since the day in the pool and it was easy to continue to do so. But look where that got him? A lump was forming in his throat. A lump the size of a golf ball. Dean could feel the wall he had meticulously constructed over the last two years start to crumble. It started with one brick, and then another, and another. Memories continued to assault Dean's mind. Painful ones, evoking emotions Dean rejected years ago. Dean's wall was tumbling down, revealing the stark truth. After his parents died he wanted to die too. He was outraged that he was left behind, alone. He wished that he had been with them and died. He continued to resist, trying desperately to put the bricks back, but no matter how many he replaced twice that amount would fall out. And then, it finally got so far ahead of Dean's efforts, he gave up. The wall crumbled completely. And Dean cried out. The pain seared his heart as if it were a branding iron. A sound, more like an animal than a human, erupted from Dean, as he tightened his hold on his folded knees. He released his grief in bursts of sobbing, screaming and punching the ground. The pain in his chest became almost unbearable. Once again he tried to put a brick back in the wall, hoping he could ease the pain. But it was too late . The pain overwhelmed him and he thought it would never end. Hot tears of anguish tracked their way down his cheeks and, reaching his chin, sat suspended, until they finished their journey down his neck. Dean sniffed and wiped this face with the back of his hands. Another sob welled up and broke free with such force Dean screamed. He raged, cried, kicked the dirt and punched the walls until he had no energy left. And, laying on the floor of the cavern, he realized why he had never dealt with his emotions. They were too big. Where could he have done what he just did without someone trying to soothe him, calm him down, or just help him? It's not that they wouldn't mean well, they would. It's more that he was never alone long enough to let go and have time to find his way back. Dean knew what had happened now. He wasn't living, he was existing. Existing with a carefully constructed wall around him for protection. He was just going through the motions. Get up, get dressed, have breakfast, go to school, go home. Home. That had changed several times since he went into foster care. There was no home anymore. The closest he'd come to feeling like he had a home was at John and Janet's.

Not because of Janet, the troll, but because of John. The way John treated Dean reminded him of his dad. But John was gone now.

Another sob found its way into Dean's throat, making it ache. He screamed out in anguish, "I MISS YOU SO MUCH MOM! I MISS YOU DAD! John, why did you leave me?!!"

His mother's smile hovered in his tormented mind, soothing his pain. His father's voice echoed once again. "Dean, don't give up son. You're almost there." Another sob was ripped from his throat. A guttural sound like that of a wounded animal, a sound Dean didn't even recognize as his own. In that moment Dean made a decision. He went from not wanting to live without his parents to needing to live in order to honor them. Again his father's voice resonated in his mind. "Dean, nothing worthwhile comes easy."

Life was worthwhile, tough sometimes, but worthwhile. Dean wiped his tear-stained face with the back of his hand, pulled the front of his T-shirt over his face, and wiped his nose with the inside of it. And smiled. His mom used to hate it when he did that! His elbow bumped into the mirror frame. He turned his head to make sure he hadn't knocked it over. And froze.

The face looking back at him was dirty, flushed, and tear stained. And....his. He'd never been so happy! He picked up the mirror, holding it in front of himself. Needing to make sure he wasn't just seeing things he made several crazy faces and watched his reflection for the mirror image. He was rewarded with a good laugh as he remembered how his parents used to love watching him do facial gymnastics. It was a gift. That's what his mom used to tell everyone. And then she would get him to perform, laughing until she cried. Another warm memory to wrap himself in when he needed comfort.

He'd forgotten all about that. He tucked the memory into his 'good memory' box so it would be there when he needed it.

It was time to get on with his life.

Chapter 21

Tom did several things while he waited for Dean. He paced, which seemed to use the energy that was making him very jittery, in a much more constructive way. He worried. Not that that was a good way to spend the bleak minutes it took for Dean to return. But it was unavoidable. A million possibilities crossed Tom's weary mind. What if he can't do what is necessary? What if there is some monster beast in there and he can't conquer it? Little did Tom know the beast Dean had to conquer was the one that lived inside him. Tom envisioned the bat headed, cricket bodied creature, of his bedtime stories, chasing Dean around the Chamber of Souls threatening to eat him! He kept looking towards the waterfall where he had last seen Dean, but the only thing there was a lot of water and an image of the dragon wavering beneath. He wished he had been able to go with his friend to help him, but he also knew that this part of the journey was Dean's to make. One thing he did know; for every person the Chamber of Souls was something different. Tailor fit, so to speak. Whatever it was that lead to the loss of your soul is what you have to confront in the Chamber of Souls. That was another tidbit of information Tom kept to himself. He didn't figure Dean needed anything extra to deal with. I wonder what Dean is dealing with in there? Tom's curiosity was starting to eat at him. Completely lost in thought and amid the thunder of the waterfall, Tom didn't hear Dean approach. So when Dean put his hand on Tom's shoulder it startled him enough to send him off the boulder yelling, "What are you doing?! You scared me half to death!" And then, recovering his brain function, he realized who was standing there. Dean. Dirty faced, tear stained, smiling, Dean.

"Dean! Are you okay? What happened in there?"

Dean answered by holding up the Liquid Mirror of Mie Self and tilting it so Tom could see. Tom's eyes rounded and then he hooted, "Yea man!" He punched the air and repeated, "Yea! I knew you could do it! You rock!"

Dean basked in the glow of his friend's praise. It was a great feeling. Tom leaned in closer to look at the mirror's frame and suddenly it disappeared. Startled, Tom said, "What the...?"

Dean knew where it was. A quick glance toward the waterfall confirmed his suspicion. The mirror was within the grasp of Eternal Change once again.

Tom followed Dean's gaze and understood. Amazing. "So...how do we get home? Ever tried to go up a water slide?"

They both knew every kid tries to go up a water slide at least once. The really determined kids try even more than once. And sometimes, a special kid comes along, who seems to have suction cups on the ends of his fingers. And when he makes it to the top all the kids who have tried and failed erupt in a cheer that can be heard for miles.

"Yep, and failed," Dean answered. "Almost broke my knee cap. You?"

"Yea, not much better here."

Then Dean remembered, he still had some magic in his pocket. He'd put it there before diving into the lake. His hand reached in and found the orb. A warm tingling started in the palm of his hand and spread to his fingertips. And he knew what he had to do.

"I have to break the orb."

"What?" Tom thought he misheard Dean. Break the orb? Dean must have lost his senses in the Chamber of Souls! That was the only way they would find their way home! Tom started to shake his head in a gesture of disbelief combined with fear. "No," he stated flatly. There was no room for negotiation in his tone, so Dean didn't bother. He raised his hand and closed his eyes.

"NO! Stop Dean! We'll never find our way home!" Tom screamed, as he lunged toward Dean to grab the orb. But he was milliseconds too late. Dean brought his hand down and released the orb onto the rocks.

"Dean, stop!" Tom repeated in the same hysterical tone. He grabbed Dean by the shoulders and continued," What are you doing?!"

Dean just smiled and said, "Trust me Tom. It's the right thing to do."

The orb shattered into what seemed like a million pieces. Each fragment sparkled and shimmered radiantly, floating on the air as if weightless. Suddenly everything around the two boys shifted. The scene around them started to melt away. Drips of color ran in rivulets down the walls to the ground. It was as if they were standing in the middle of a painting that was dissolving around them. The two boys just stood silently and watched. Slowly, the scene before them changed to something they recognized. Dean's foster home.

Wordlessly, the two boys looked at each other and burst out laughing. Two high fives later, they were still laughing. Incredulous around how they got there, they didn't notice the voice until it repeated the question. "Where have you been?"

Dean recognized that voice. Dean missed that voice. It was John. "Dean, where have you been? I've been looking for you. It's after six. Janet said you left the house for school this morning and she hasn't seen you since. Dean? Did you hear me?"

Dean just stood glued to his spot. His eyes, however, were glued to the flames licking their way over John's shoulder. Dean remembered very clearly what those flames engulfed on John's back. The dragon from the Sea of Flames. Dean admired it every time he was lucky enough to see it. John rarely removed his shirt unless he was out in the yard doing chores. It was magnificent. Now he understood John's mysterious comments whenever Dean asked about the tattoo.

"Ya, I heard you John." Then he remembered. "What are you doing here?"

John looked at the ground and Dean's heart skipped a beat. John raised his head and looked directly into Dean's eyes. "I came to get you."

"Me? What do you mean?" Dean's heart skipped another beat.

"It took me longer than I thought it would, but now it is all done." John started. "If you are okay with it, that is."

"Okay with what?"

"I applied to be your foster parent." He bent down, putting his face within inches of Dean's, and caught his eyes....and held them, as he said, "Just me Dean. You and me. I got the approval this morning. That's why I've been looking for you all day. I want to help you pack your things."

Dean was stunned. He couldn't believe his ears. It had only been one day! And John was here to get him. Dean was awash with emotion. "That would be great, and later, boy do I have a story for you."

Cast of Characters

- Soul Master: a large creature with the head and wings of a bat and the body and appendages of a cricket, that sits on the King's Throne at the entrance of the Chamber of Souls.

Stalactite: Hangs down from the ceiling of the cave and is formed from ground water filtering through the earth's layers and dripping through the cave ceiling. The minerals contained in the water are deposited as the water evaporates. It takes hundreds of years to form one.

Stalagmite: A formation which builds upwards from a cave floor as a result of mineral deposits contained in water dripping from the ceiling of the cave. They are usually located beneath a stalactite.

Lifeline: A crack in the ceiling of a cave through which water drips or slowly flows. It produces speleothems (general term for cave formations) in a cave.

Columns: are formed when stalactites and stalagmites meet or when one grows all the way to floor or ceiling.

Cave Drapes: made by water flowing down the side of a stalactite instead of evenly down all sides of the formation. They are extremely fast growing, three times faster than the stalactite. They are also called Elephant Ears or Tobacco Leaves.

Flowstones: sheet like deposits of calcite that form where water flows down walls or along floors of the caves.

Soda Straws: hollow formations that hang from the ceiling that look like soda straws.

Cave Bacon: flowstone that has a beige and brown color in layers that are so thin and wide that when light hits them it looks exactly like sheets of bacon. It usually has a curving nature.

Carrots Patch or Worms Eye View of Carrots Patch: formations that are usually in large patches on the ceiling of the cave and resemble the underside of a carrot patch.

Cave Popcorn: knob-like appearance, the most common formation and found in a variety of locations. Not sure exactly how it is formed because of its different locations. Can even be found in small crawl spaces and forms easily.

Cave Coral: comes in a variety of colors. White is the most beautiful.

Rimstone Dams: deposits of minerals that form around pools of water.

Helecites: the most delicate and beautiful cave formations, they are curving or angular in form. Also called butterflies, curly fries, or clumps of worms.

Cool Cavern Facts

1. _Lechuguilla Cave_: The deepest limestone cave and fourth longest in the United States known as the Jewel of the Underground and located in Carlsbad, New Mexico.

2. _Forbidden Caverns_: Complete with towering natural chimneys, grottos, crystal clear stream, spring water, onyx and dripstones.

3. _The Kings Throne_: Looks like a chair draped in flowstones or draperies.

4. _Mystic Cavern_: In the heart of the Ozark Mountains on North West Arkansas. The Crystal Dome was found 100 years after Mystic, but its entrance is only 400 feet away.

5. _De Soto Caverns_: Found in Alabama, they were used as Indian burial grounds. Excavation unearthed a 2000 year old Indian burial, now on display. There is a lazer

light show in the great Onyx Cathedral. The main room is twelve stories high and larger than a football field.

6. *Blue Springs Caverns*: Found in Indiana. The Myst'ry River flows through the caverns and are only accessible only by boat.

7. *Squire Boone Caverns*: Also in Indiana. It was discovered by Squire and Daniel Boone over 200 years ago and has rivers and underground waterfalls.

8. *Cave of the Mounds*: Wisconsin's Oldest Classroom, also referred to as *the jewel box of Americas' major caves*. Acidic water dissolved the 400 million year old limestone bedrock. It has a constant temperature of 50 degrees Fahrenheit.

9. *Endless Caverns*: New Market Virginia. Discovered in 1879, located on the side of Massanutten Mountain, overlooking the Shenandoah Valley. They found aWoolly Mammoth tooth there.

10. *Inner Space Cavern*: Found in Texas and was discovered by the Texas Highway Department. Started out in narrow tunnels that get narrower and then opens into beautiful rooms The Straw Room is full of soda straws.

11. *The Lost Sea*: Guiness Book of World Records has it as the largest underground lake of sweet water located in Craighead Caverns in Tennessee. Cherokee artifacts, like pottery, arrowheads, weapons and jewelry were found in the cave. The tracks of a Pleistoncene jaguar were found deep inside. It was discovered in 1905 by a thirteen-year-old boy who wiggled through a tiny, muddy opening 300 feet underground and found a huge room half filled with water. The room was so large that his light was swallowed up by the darkness long before reaching the far wall or ceiling. For the rest of his life, the boy, Sands, delighted in describing how he threw mud balls as far as he could into the blackness

and heard nothing but splashes. There seems to be no end to the lake. Divers armed with sonar equipment have gone into the rooms filled with water that are beneath the lake and have not found anything but more water.

12. ***Meramec Caverns***: Missouri.....local Indian tribes used them as shelter. 1700, the cave's natural resource, saltpeter, a mineral used in gunpowder, was discovered by a French miner. Used in gunpowder. The cavern was used as a station on the ***Underground Railroad*** to hide escaping slaves. 1870's Jessie James and his band used the cavern as a hide out. There are twenty six miles of underground passages and seven upper levels.

13. ***Bracken Cave***: Austin, Texas....20 million bats zoom outside to feed on insects every summer night.

14. ***Vietnam Cave***: Phong Nha-Ke Bang National Park, near the border with Laos. It is an infinite cave that has a jungle inside.

Did You Know.....

- The oil from the human touch damages formations because it causes water to avoid an area, which stops the mineral deposits.

- Limestone and other minerals are the deposits.

- Bacteria lives in underground streams.

- Fungi thrives in a stable, dark cave environment.

- Bat poop is called guano and provides food for tiny organisms like bacteria and fungi.

- A group of bats is called a colony.

- Baby bats are called pups.

- Five hundred baby bats live crammed into a one square foot space. Their bodies create the warmth needed to keep comfortable.

- Mexican Free-tailed bats can fly up to 60 miles (97 kilometers) an hour with the help of tail winds. They go as high as 10,000 feet (3048 meters), up where planes fly. No other kind of bat in the world forms such large colonies.

- Bats made a contribution to the Civil War: In 1863, a gun powder factory was built in Texas that got a key ingredient, saltpeter, from bat guano.

- Troglobites are cave dwelling creatures that navigate without eyes, go for weeks or months without food, and can live for more than a century. Examples are: millepedes, spiders, worms, blind salamanders, and eyeless fish. The crayfish of Shelta Cave in Alabama may reproduce when 100 years old and live to 175.

- Troglobites have no need of pigment or vision. Instead they have elaborate appendages and beefed-up nerve centers to interpret slight air-pressure or temperature changes, sounds, and smells.

- The first foot-long salamanders found in Slovenian caves were first thought to be baby dragons.

All Things Magical

Magical Object Index

Flaming Pearl: A pearl, encapsulated in blue flame, that rests within the claws of the Sea of Flames Dragon. It represents spiritual perfection. An amulet of luck that the Ancients believe symbolizes the most precious treasure — wisdom. When placed properly the Flaming Pearl can multiply any inanimate object it touches.

Longuu Oracle: A piece of tortoise shell strung with a rope of silver thread and bound by a magical knot that hangs around the neck of the Bone Yard Dragon. It is a spiritual script, carved by the ancients that recorded historical events. Also sometimes called 'dragon bones'. When used for divination, the shell is placed into a hot fire. The cracks created by the heat are read by the ancients and are believed to be predictions of the future and warnings of peril.

Liquid Mirror of Mie-Self: A mirror of water that is contained by a white coral frame and rests in the arms of the Lost Sea of Inner Space Dragon. The Ancients believe the mirror holds the key to attaining the Inner World of Light. The mirror has the ability, when used properly, to capture a lost soul and return it to its owner, but demands a sacrifice and the courage to face your deepest, innermost truth. The Liquid Mirror of Mie-Self represents the true self.

Magical Charm Index

The Silver Orb: Emits moon rays that have been captured and contained within the orb. It creates a soft, tingling feeling where it touches flesh when it is connected with its holder. It offers subtle influence and emotional guidance.

The Living Bean: When used with intent, the bean reflects the user's thoughts and feelings. If the user cannot channel their thoughts and harness their energy, the result can be catastrophic.

The Iyc Crystal: An iridescent crystal, in the shape of an icicle, that, when used with intent, turns anything it touches to ice.

Dragon Index

Dragons symbolize **the spirit of the way,** bringing eternal change. The early Chinese believed in four magical, spiritual and benevolent animals; the Dragon, the Phoenix, the Tortoise and the Unicorn. The Dragon was the most revered. Dragon fire represents the soul's spark of light, emanating from the flame of creation.

The Sea of Flames Dragon: A cobalt blue dragon with diamond eyes that sits amid the Sea of Flames in the first cavern and holds the Flaming Pearl within its claws.

The Bone Yard Dragon: A cobalt blue dragon with deep, amber eyes that resides under the stone slabs in the center of the Bone Yard and only rises when the riddle of the stones has been solved and said aloud.

The Lost Sea of Inner Space Dragon: A cobalt blue dragon with sapphire eyes that is concealed within the waterfall that feeds the Lost Sea. There is an underwater passage that leads to the cave behind the Dragon.

Epilogue

The shadow within a shadow stirred. It could feel The Energy it had wrapped within its darkness gaining power. It tried, without success, to consume each escaping sparkle, desperate to keep the Energy within the Eternal Darkness. The struggle continued until finally the Energy burst forth, eliminating the darkness once again.

With a roar of defeat the shadow retreated into the Eternal Darkness to wait.

The Beginning

Acknowledgements

Many thanks, in many forms, must go out to many people.

First, and foremost; Dr. Omahen: for saving my life and making it possible to finish what I started.

Sandy and Jasmine; for edit expertise and hours of time.

Jasmine, for suggesting I self publish, and pointing me in the right direction.

Noreen; for wanting more.

This book is dedicated to David, my husband of nearly forty years; the person who unfailingly stood by my side when all seemed lost. He nursed me, protected me, and ultimately, believed in me. Without his strength, love, and unending support, I never would have made it to the finish line.

Love You Baby.....

Made in the USA
Charleston, SC
14 August 2014